BLUE STEELE - BOUNTY HUNTER

BOOK 1 OF THE BLUE STEELE SERIES

REMINGTON KANE

Year Zero Publishing

INTRODUCTION

BLUE STEELE – BOUNTY HUNTER
Book 1 of the Blue Steele Series

When murder suspect Vincent Caine jumps bail, Blue decides to hunt him down for the ten-thousand-dollar bounty

However, when Caine's guilt comes into question, Blue keeps searching for the man, and not only for the bounty. She wants answers.

Who really killed Vincent Caine's wife? Was it her lover, or is Caine far more devious than even the police suspect?

In the end, Blue discovers the truth and learns that the human heart holds many secrets.

ACKNOWLEDGMENTS

I write for you.

—Remington Kane

# PART ONE

BLUE STEELE

CHAPTER 1

It was a Friday night, and I was on yet another blind date. At least this one was cute.

He had blue/green eyes, curly blond hair and smelled great. His name was William Grant, and he was an architect, thirty-two, divorced, no children. William, Billy as he liked to be called, was clean-shaven, articulate, and well read.

We were in Fort Worth, Texas, at a restaurant called *The Round-up*. The décor was western and the dress code, casual. I was wearing my best boots along with a blue dress that hung three inches above my knees. I was also displaying a tasteful bit of cleavage, well, all right, it was an ample bit of cleavage. But hey, they're one of my best features and I never met a man who disliked looking at them.

I was having a good time, and that's when Mickey Kyle walked into the restaurant. Mickey was a lifelong thug who skipped bail three weeks ago and now had a four-thousand-dollar bounty on his head.

Mickey walked up to the bar and spoke to the

bartender for a moment. She reached under the counter and brought out a large paper bag. Take-out, Mickey was picking up a take-out order.

"Billy," I said.

"Yes?"

"Do you remember I told you I was a bounty hunter?"

He smiled, did I mention that he had a great smile, well he did.

"Of course, I remember. Why do you ask?"

"Because I have to go to work now, see that man at the bar, the one with the white bag in his hand? His name is Mickey Kyle and he's worth four thousand dollars to whoever brings him in."

Billy turned his head and stared at Mickey. Mickey Kyle was forty, stood six-foot-four, and weighed nearly three hundred pounds. At the time, he was wearing a sleeveless T-shirt that displayed his many and varied tattoos. He was also bearded, and his broad nose hooked a little to the right, while his beady eyes had a mean slant to them.

Billy turned back to me with a look of puzzlement.

"You're calling the cops, right? I mean you're not going to try to arrest him yourself, are you?"

"Mickey is all mine; I've been looking for him for weeks."

I opened my purse and grabbed a pen just as Mickey left the bar. I then hastily scribbled my number on Billy's palm.

"I had a great time, call me?"

Billy nodded as he stared at his hand, and I rushed out of the restaurant while searching my purse for my truck keys. When I reached the parking lot, luck was with me. Mickey was standing outside the restaurant talking to a redheaded woman with too much make-up and shoes I wouldn't be caught dead in. I mean, who wears open-back shoes?

They were standing by a motorcycle that I assumed was Mickey's, but a few moments later, the redhead straddled the bike and rode off. With a gun in my right hand and cuffs in my left, I walked over toward Mickey and smiled.

"Hello, Mickey, nice night huh?"

Mickey looked at the gun and the handcuffs and then stared at me. He didn't begin laughing until his eyes found mine.

"Are you kidding me? You think your skinny little girl ass is gonna take me in? The damn cops must be getting desperate if there hiring chippies now."

"I'm not a cop; I'm a bounty hunter." I tossed the cuffs to him. "Put those on."

He made no move to catch the cuffs; they hit him on the chest and fell to the ground. They were followed by the bag of food, as a second later, he was charging at me. I stood my ground, took careful aim, and pulled the trigger.

I carried a thirty-eight with a two-inch barrel. My gun had a short barrel because it made it easier to carry and I rarely needed it for distance. If I ever had to shoot a target more than a dozen yards away, the gun would have been next to useless.

Mickey was six feet away when I shot him in the left knee. He fell at my side, moaning.

The sound of the shot brought the restaurant crowd outside and I spotted Billy standing near the front. His eyes were wide, and he looked frightened. A moment later, a man pushed past him and headed over to me.

The man was holding a badge in one hand and a gun in the other. His name was Deke Thomas; he was a Texas Ranger. Deke was John Wayne tough and tall, and even looked a little like ol' Duke. Deke had been a friend of my father's and I went to school with his oldest daughter, Jenna.

Deke looked down at Mickey and then over at me.

"Hey, Blue, is that Mickey Kyle?"

"Yep."

"He's worth what, three grand?"

"Four grand."

While we talked, Mickey moaned, and I do believe I saw tears in his manly eyes.

"Shot him in the knee, huh?"

"He called me a chippie and charged at me."

"Well, judging by the look of that knee, I'd say his charging days are over."

A police cruiser arrived, and Deke talked to the cops getting out of it. I looked back at the crowd, searching for Billy. He was nowhere in sight.

When all the dust settled, I arrived back home at 2:23 a.m. and fell into bed with a splitting headache.

Billy never called me.

Maybe I should have shot him in the knee too.

CHAPTER 2

A FEW DAYS LATER, BECCA AND I WERE OUT FOR A RUN IN Trinity Park.

Becca was my best friend and had been such for as long as I could remember. Her family and mine were neighbors and we were born only two days apart. Becca is a natural blonde with brown eyes, who these days wears her hair short. She says that with five kids under the age of ten, she has no time for worrying about her hair.

My hair is dark and my eyes green. I wear my hair long, always have, and even if I had five kids I would still do so. I am vain when it comes to my hair.

We were both wearing shorts with tank tops, and we were both sweating from head to toe. It was a miserably humid day in Fort Worth and the temperature, at eleven a.m., was already in the eighties. We came to a stop near the Mark Twain statue and caught our breath.

"Are you working today?" Becca said.

"Yeah, a man by the name of Vincent Caine jumped bail yesterday; he's an accountant, the bounty is ten grand."

"What did he do?"

"He murdered his wife."

Becca made a face. "Must you always go after the dangerous ones? Doesn't anybody ever skip bail for not paying their parking tickets?"

I smiled. Becca worried about me more than my mother did.

"I'll be careful, and I'll be ten thousand dollars richer when I find him."

"You're really determined to buy a ranch someday, aren't you?"

"Not someday, by the time I'm forty, and I'm well ahead of schedule."

"That Vermont trip really paid off, huh?"

"Yeah," I said, and smiled. A few months ago, in Vermont, I was tracking a fugitive named Sebastian Rojo. I didn't get Rojo due to... unusual circumstances, but I did get the hundred grand in uncut diamonds he was carrying.

Becca walked over and stared at me. "Do you still think about him?"

"About who?"

"Don't play dumb, Blue, not with me."

I nodded. "Yeah, I still think about him. You would too if you had met him. But, hell, he's married; I mean he's *really* married."

While in Vermont, I met a man named... well, his name doesn't matter, but he was unlike anyone I had ever known. Sebastian Rojo had taken his wife, Dr. Jessica White, as a hostage to make his escape. I teamed up with the doctor's husband to rescue his wife and capture Rojo. We got his wife back and I wound up with Rojo's diamonds.

Becca reached out and gave my hand a squeeze. "I'm

sorry, baby, but you'll find the right guy someday, ya know?"

"Like you did? You and Richie have been together since the eighth grade. Do you know how lucky you are?"

Becca grinned shyly, "Yeah, I do."

∼

I SPENT THE NEXT FEW DAYS TALKING TO ANYONE WHO knew anything about Vincent Caine, his neighbors, relatives, clients. I learned two things. One, most of the people in his life didn't believe that he killed his wife, and two, most of them didn't like his wife.

Lucinda Caine, Vincent's dead wife, was described as selfish by many who knew her. She had been fifteen years younger than her husband, and some thought that the age difference had been part of the problem. I was told that she cheated on her husband, gambled them into bankruptcy and refused to get a job to help dig them out of it. In fact, Lucinda Caine seemed so universally disliked that I sought out the one person who should have something positive to say about her, her mother.

Bobbi Reed, Lucinda's mother, lived in Dallas with Lucinda's little sister, Rachel. The house turned out to be a double-wide trailer in a mobile home park off interstate 30.

No one was home when I got there, and so I sat on the trailer's steps and waited. Sitting in the weeds near the trailer, was an old Volkswagen Beetle that looked like little more than a pile of rust. There were weeds surrounding it, but I noticed that the weeds in front, by the trunk, looked trampled, as if someone had been standing there recently. The trailer too was sunbaked and had paint chipping off.

The trailer had seen better days and so had Bobbi Reed.

Bobbi Reed was forty-four but looked at least sixty. I caught her coming home from work on the night shift at the hospital; she was a nurse. Her daughter Rachel was with her and was quite a contrast. Rachel Reed was sixteen, shapely, and had about the biggest blue eyes I'd ever seen, while her curly blonde hair fell about her dimpled cheeks.

The three of us sat around the living room with the TV on, but the sound turned down. I was sipping on a cup of coffee that was surprisingly good and listening to Bobbi Reed tell me about her oldest daughter.

"She was a saint, a saint to put up with that man," Bobbi Reed said.

"Why do you say that? What did Vincent do to her?"

"He treated Lucinda like property and wouldn't spend any money on her. The man owned an accounting firm for God's sake; he must have been rolling in money."

"Did you know he filed for bankruptcy recently?"

"That was just a trick to fool the IRS; believe me, Vincent Caine is devious."

"Maybe, but the police think he killed your daughter to collect on her life insurance because he was desperate to get out of debt."

"He's greedy, that's all. He used my poor daughter from the moment he met her. Did you know she was only fourteen when they met?"

I raised an eyebrow. "No, I hadn't heard that."

"Lucinda swore to me that nothing went on between them until she married him at eighteen, but I'm not a complete fool. Plus, there was that trouble with the neighbor girl."

"That was just a misunderstanding, Mom," Rachel Reed said.

I looked over at her. "What was a misunderstanding?"

"Lucinda and Vincent had a neighbor woman with a teenage daughter," Bobbi said. "Lucinda told me that she caught the girl leaving their house one day when she came home earlier than expected. The girl was attractive and looked older than she was, but she was only fifteen for God's sake."

"What did the girl say?"

"She told Lucinda that she had just stopped by to talk to Vincent about donating money toward new band uniforms."

"That's possible, isn't it?"

"The girl had never been in the band. If she was playing an instrument that day, it was a skin flute."

"Mom!" Rachel said, while I laughed, despite the seriousness of it all.

"What did Lucinda do next?"

"She told the girl's mother about her suspicions; not long after, the girl and her mother moved away. Can you imagine having to tell another woman that your husband may have been fooling around with her child? Lucinda said their marriage was never the same after that."

"How long ago did this happen?"

"A few years ago."

"If she believed he was a child molester, then why did she stay with him?"

"I hate Vincent for killing my daughter, but there is one thing about him I can't deny, the man's a charmer, always was and always will be. Despite his faults, Lucinda loved him."

The doubt I harbored at that statement must have shown on my face, because Bobbi frowned at me.

"Let me guess, people have been telling you about Lucinda's affairs? Well, it's true, but they weren't affairs, it was just one man, Harold Weidman. He was Lucinda's dentist and he wanted her to leave Vincent and live with him."

"Why didn't she?"

Bobbi shrugged. "Vincent charmed her out of it, said he was a changed man. Two weeks later, she was dead."

As I was leaving the trailer, I stopped at the bottom of the steps and asked Bobbi one last question.

"You say that Vincent met your daughter when she was only fourteen, how did they meet?"

Bobbi Reed stared at me a while before answering.

"Back then… Vincent was my boyfriend."

And then, she slowly shut the door.

CHAPTER 3

Dr. Harold Weidman had a dental practice in a Fort Worth office building that was a short walk away from the Kimbell Art Museum.

After I explained who I was and why I was there, the doctor agreed to speak with me. We spoke in one of the examination rooms. The antiseptic smell of the place and the sight of the drills made my teeth itch. I hate visiting the dentist.

Dr. Weidman was a pleasant looking man. He was in his mid-thirties and had short brown hair with gray eyes seated behind a pair of round glasses.

"You say you're a bounty hunter, Miss Steele? That's an unusual profession for a young woman, no?"

I smiled, while hoping he spotted no flaws in my teeth. "I'm a Bail Enforcement Agent, and there are a few of us, doctor. Now please, tell me everything you know about Lucinda and Vincent Caine."

"About Vincent, I know almost nothing, about Lucinda… it would take a year."

"You loved her?"

"Oh yes, from the moment I laid eyes on her."

"Do you believe that Vincent killed her?"

He shook his head slowly. "I don't know, probably, or else why would he have fled?"

"Did Lucinda ever mention a place that Vincent might run to, such as a childhood friend, or a relative that he was particularly close to?"

The doctor stared at me. "We spoke of him as little as possible."

"Yes, of course."

"The police have asked me all of this already; do you really think you'll locate him before they can?"

"Yes doctor, I do."

"Why?"

"Because I have ten thousand more reasons to find him then they do."

~

NEXT, I PAID A VISIT TO *GOLDMAN, HARPER, ROGERS & Dent*. They were the law firm that was representing Vincent Caine. I had little hope of getting anyone to talk to me, but in my business, you took things as they came. Talking to Caine's attorney could only shed light on where he might have gone, and so I tried to get a few words in with the man.

To my great shock, I was ushered into Gary Dent's office in less than a minute. Gary Dent was younger than I expected, and a hunk. He was six-feet tall and slim, with wavy dark hair and a cleft chin.

As his assistant escorted me into the office, I watched as Dent's eyes took me in from tip to tail. Normally, I wore jeans when working, but lazy girl that I am, I hadn't gotten around to doing the laundry for a while and all my jeans were dirty. So today, I was wearing a black silk skirt with a white blouse and a pair of turquoise boots that rode up to mid-calf. As I sat and crossed my legs, Dent's eyes widened in interest.

He held up my business card. "A Private Investigator? I thought you were a Bail Enforcement Agent, a Bounty Hunter."

"I'm all three actually; I was a PI and later became a Bounty Hunter, but it's the law in Texas that bounty hunters must also have a PI license, as I'm sure you know."

He shook his head. "Actually, no, I didn't know that; but now I'll never forget it." Then, he smiled, and I felt my heart go aflutter. I am such a sucker for a great smile, and also humility. A lawyer admitting that he didn't know everything was a first for me.

"The reason I'm here, Mr. Dent—"

"Gary, call me Gary, and you're Blue. Is that really your name, Blue Steele?"

"Yes, my father was expecting a boy."

"Thank God he was disappointed," Gary said, and then he smiled again.

"Thank you for the compliment, Gary, but I'm here to talk about Vincent Caine."

At the mention of Caine, Gary Dent grimaced.

"You don't like Mr. Caine?" I asked.

"Vinnie? Yeah, I like him. No, I just made that face because I'm so pissed at Vinnie for running off. He had zero chance of going to prison for his wife's murder."

I uncrossed my legs and leaned forward. "Why do you say that?"

"He didn't do it and we could prove it. The timeline was all wrong. Vinnie is a smoker; he likes cigars. At the time his wife was being murdered, he was at a store buying some. We have three witnesses that can place him there, plus the store's security camera."

"He was at the store at the exact time his wife was killed?"

"Well, not the exact time, but it was only twenty minutes afterward that the neighbor swears he heard the gunshot that killed Lucinda, and the cigar shop is a forty-five-minute drive away, so, unless Vinnie learned to fly, he's innocent."

"He could have hired someone to kill his wife."

"Yes, but if he had done that, wouldn't he have given himself more leeway on the alibi?"

"All right, then why would he run at all?"

Gary smiled at me again. If he kept doing that, I was going to leap over the desk and molest him.

"I'm not at liberty to say, Blue; attorney-client privilege, you know?"

I thought for a moment, and the answer came to me.

"Money, he was hiding money from the IRS, and when he got indicted for murder, all of his financial dealings came to light." I grinned. "He could actually receive a longer sentence for tax evasion than for murder; that would be a reason to run."

Gary squinted at me. "You're a smart one, Blue; I'll have to remember that."

"Vincent Caine was planning on divorcing his wife and leaving her with nothing, so he told anyone who would listen that she was gambling him into bankruptcy. Then, after the divorce was final, he would suddenly make a financial recovery."

"Let's say that hypothetically that was the truth, does that sound like a man planning to kill his wife?"

"No, it sounds like a man planning to cheat her, not kill her."

"Exactly."

"So then, who killed Lucinda Caine?"

"My guess? It was dear old Mom."

"Bobbi Reed?"

"I'm not just Vinnie's lawyer. We've been friends since college. I was there when he married Lucinda. Bobbi Reed was nowhere in sight. Vinnie met Lucinda while he was dating Bobbi, and then they broke up. A few years later, Vinnie marries Lucinda out of the blue. A suspicious man, or woman, might believe that Vinnie and Lucinda had never lost contact."

"Even though she was just a child?"

"He swore to me at the time that he had never touched her and that she was a virgin on their wedding night."

"Did you believe him?"

"I thought I did, but when he contacted me after being charged with murder, I realized I hadn't kept in touch with him since the wedding, so, maybe not."

"But why would Bobbi Reed kill her own daughter?"

"Jealousy, Vinnie told me that Bobbi and Lucinda barely spoke for years, even though Lucinda's little sister stayed with her from time to time. Vinnie said that Bobbi used them as free babysitters, but other than that, she wanted nothing to do with them. Then, six months ago, Bobbi offered an olive branch and she and Lucinda became best friends. You know what they say: Keep your friends close, and your enemies even closer."

"Still, her own daughter?"

"Or rival, I guess it depends on how you look at it."

"So, your theory is that Bobbi Reed killed her own daughter to frame Vincent Caine? I don't know; let's say it's true, why now?"

"I take it you've met Bobbi Reed?"

"Yes, this morning."

"Not exactly the picture of health, is she?"

"What are you saying?"

"Bobbi Reed has terminal liver cancer. According to what my investigator found out, she's got maybe six months to live. If she wanted to get back at Vinnie and Lucinda, now was the only time she had."

∼

When I was leaving, Gary escorted me to the elevator.

"How old are you, Blue?"

"I'm twenty-eight, why?"

"I'm forty, too old?"

I had several thoughts then. One was serious, one was evasive, and three were just plain wiseass, but in the end, I simply answered, "No."

"Good, so I'll call you soon?"

"Yes."

He gave me his best smile yet, and then the elevator arrived, and we said goodbye.

CHAPTER 4

I WAS IN MY OFFICE, WHICH IS ALSO MY TRUCK, A FORD F150 that had more miles on it than I cared to think about. My truck was black with a tan interior. I had owned it since the day I got my driver's license. It had been a birthday gift from my father.

I was invited to have dinner with Becca and her family. My phone rang as I pulled into their driveway. I looked at the caller ID and saw that it was Ron, owner of the AAAAAAAAAA Bail Bonds Company. He used the ten As to be sure he was listed first in the yellow pages, but most people just referred to his company as Ten A, which was funny, because Ron's last name was Tenney.

"Hi Ron, what's up?"

"Blue, baby, how's my favorite bloodhound?"

"Good, how about you?"

"I'm good, kid, but listen, I got an easy one for you, and it pays three grand."

I straightened in my seat as Becca and Richie came out to greet me. Behind them poured out their brood, three girls and two boys, ages two to nine. I held up an index finger and Becca stopped in her tracks, as Richie told the kids to hush.

"What is it, Ron?"

"A guy by the name of Felix Porta, he skipped a few weeks ago on multiple B&E charges. I got a reliable tip that he's working under the table at the Easy Wax Car Wash, you know, the one on May Street? Come see me and pick up the paper, then go grab Felix, the whole thing should only take a few hours."

"And you say he's worth three grand?" I said, then watched as Becca's face fell. I had blown off the last two invitations to dinner because of work and it looked like I was going to do it again.

"Yeah, three bills, so how soon can you get here?"

I climbed out of my truck and sent Becca a smile. "Thanks for thinking of me first, Ron, but I'll have to pass; I'm having dinner with my family."

~

I LEFT BECCA'S THAT NIGHT FEELING GOOD AND A LITTLE wistful that I didn't have a family of my own yet. Maybe someday.

On the ride home, an idea came to me in a flash, and I pulled over to make a call.

"Hello?"

"Hi, Mrs. Reed, this is Miss Steele, do you remember me?"

"Of course, you're that bounty hunter."

"Right, could I ask you a few more questions, ma'am?"

"Yes but be quick about it; I'm just about to leave for work."

I was quick, and she answered all my questions. After an hour of searching through county records on my laptop, I thought I knew where Vincent Caine was hiding.

~

THE FIFTEEN-YEAR-OLD NEIGHBOR GIRL THAT LUCINDA suspected her husband of molesting was now a nineteen-year-old adult. Her name was Sarah Miller.

Sarah lived in a tiny first-floor apartment on Lafayette Street in Dallas. I arrived there just after ten o'clock. It was a humid night, and as soon as I left the air-conditioned comfort of my truck, a slick of perspiration began to appear on my forehead.

At the curb, I spotted the SUV registered in Sarah Miller's name. I peeked in a side window and saw that the back seat was loaded with cardboard boxes. It looked like Sarah was planning on moving, likely out of state, and possibly with a fugitive boyfriend in tow.

I headed up the walkway, and that's when I heard the shots. One shot, then a pause, and then five more, six in all.

It sounded like a thirty-eight revolver. I whipped my own gun out and ran toward the front door. It was locked. Just then, a neighbor stuck his head out a second story window.

"Call the police," I said. "Tell them that shots have been fired and that there may be a fugitive on the premises."

The man nodded, and I heard a woman's voice, although I couldn't make out the words.

The man yelled down to me. "My wife says that someone dressed in black just ran out the back door."

I walked around the building with my gun held level with both hands and my eyes scanning left to right. I had to fight the urge to rush to the back yard as quickly as I could. Often, moving fast is no good, it's better to go slow and be careful. As I made the turn at the back, I spotted a shaft of light beaming into the back yard; it was coming from an open doorway.

I approached cautiously, as I kept one eye on the doorway while scanning the shadows to my right. The neighbor saw someone run out the back door, but that didn't have to mean they ran away. They could just as easily be hiding.

I peeked into the apartment and saw a kitchen. There was water running in the sink and a small stack of dirty dishes beside it. I let the water run and went farther into the apartment. I didn't have to go very far; they were in the next room.

Vincent Caine and Sarah Miller were both lying dead on the living room floor. Scattered around them were more cardboard boxes, some were full and taped shut, while others were empty.

Sarah had been shot in the forehead once, while Vincent had four distinct wounds in his bare chest. A fifth wound was in a different location. If the bloodstain spreading across his boxers was any indication, Caine had died a falsetto.

CHAPTER 5

A PATROL CAR RESPONDED, AND I TOLD THEM MY STORY. As I waited for the homicide detectives to show, my phone rang.

"Hello?"

"Blue, hi, it's Gary Dent. I hope I'm not calling at too late an hour?"

"No, Gary, it's just… listen, I've got some bad news. Vincent Caine is dead, murdered."

"Oh my God, Vinnie… Blue, who killed him?"

"I don't know. I only heard the shots."

"You were there when it happened?"

"Yes, I tracked him down at his girlfriend's apartment, but I got here too late."

"Too late? Any earlier and you might have been murdered too. Tell me where you are, and I'll be right there."

"Right, sorry. I should have told you already, after all, Caine was your client."

"Screw Vinnie; I'm coming there to be with you."

And with a smile on my face, I told him the address.

~

Gary arrived just as the cops were finishing with me. He walked over and gave me a kiss on the cheek.

"Thank God you're all right."

"I'm fine, and I'm sorry about Caine, I know that at one time he was a good friend of yours."

He nodded. "Yeah, thanks, so tell me, who was the girlfriend?"

"Her name was Sarah Miller; it looks like they were about to run off together. She lived next door to Caine when she was fifteen, apparently, they, eh, kept in touch."

"Jesus, Blue, another teenybopper? Oh Vinnie, you sick bastard."

I took his hand and looked into his eyes. "I have something to tell you; I think this might all be my fault."

"What do you mean?"

"Earlier tonight, I recalled the story Bobbi Reed told me about Caine's rumored affair with a teenage neighbor. I then wondered if maybe he had kept in touch with the girl, and if he did, she might even know where he was hiding."

Gary lifted my hand to his lips and kissed it. "You're very clever, Blue; I may have to put you on retainer as an investigator. The guy I had looking for Vinnie would have never thought to look here."

"It was a hunch, but I didn't know the girl's name or even which house the girl had lived in, and so I called—"

"Bobbi Reed, you called Bobbi Reed and she put two and two together and came here and killed Vinnie."

"Possibly, I don't know, but I told the police about her and they're going to talk to her."

Gary cupped my face in his hands. "Nothing here is your fault. Bobbi, or whoever killed Vinnie, is to blame; you got that?"

I smiled. "I got it."

"Good, now let's get out of here."

∽

WE DROVE TO A DINER AND HAD COFFEE. IN BETWEEN SIPS, we talked a little about ourselves.

I learned that Gary had married just after college, but that the marriage hadn't even lasted a year.

"So, you've never been married, Blue?"

"No."

"Ever come close?"

"Once, but… it doesn't matter."

"Hmm, it sounds like there's a story there, but I won't pry. So, tell me, what gets you going other than catching bad guys?"

I smiled. "Horses."

"Horses? What kind?"

"Quarter horses."

"Oh, you like the quarter milers, the fast ones, eh?"

"Yes, but I love any kind of horse; by the way, do you ride?"

"Not only do I ride, but I own a ranch."

I blinked. "I'm sorry, what did you say?"

"I said I own a cattle ranch, the triple Q, in Bandera."

"You own a ranch? Wait, Bandera is about three hundred miles away. You must not get there too often."

"No, I fly there about every other weekend, in my Cessna."

"You own a ranch *and* an airplane?"

"Yes."

"Jesus, Gary, are you rich?"

"I inherited the ranch from my grandfather. I own it with my brother and sister, who both live there, and the plane, well, that's my toy."

"You're a rich rancher; that's who I want to be when I grow up."

He glanced down at my breasts. "You look fully grown to me."

"Only on the outside, on the inside I'm a kid who wants to spend her life around horses."

"So, why don't you?"

"I want them to be my horses, on my ranch."

"Is that your dream?"

"Yeah, what's yours?"

He stared into my eyes. "I want to meet the right woman."

~

WE WERE OUTSIDE IN THE DINER PARKING LOT, SAYING goodbye as we stood beside our vehicles.

Gary had an F-150 too, although his was red and much newer than mine.

"Goodnight, Blue, I guess we could call this a first date maybe?"

I shook my head. "Dinner is a date, not just coffee."

"Well then, dinner it is, are you busy Saturday night?"

"No, and I look forward to it."

A moment later and we were kissing. When our lips parted, we both smiled.

As I drove home, my phone rang. It was Gary.

"Missed me already?"

"As a matter of fact, yes, but I have something to tell

you. Dr. Harold Weidman, Lucinda's lover? The police just arrested him for Vinnie's murder."

I swung my truck into a tight U-turn and headed downtown. It looked like it was going to be a long night.

CHAPTER 6

THE DETECTIVES THAT WERE HANDLING LUCINDA'S MURDER were also working the Vincent Caine and Sarah Miller murders, since the assumption was that they were connected.

They located Bobbi Reed at Parkland Memorial, where she said she had been since her shift started. When they told her about Caine's death, she smiled. They left the hospital, unconvinced of her innocence, but also unable to prove her involvement. They hoped to clear things up once they had a chance to study the hospital's surveillance video.

Next, they went to see Dr. Weidman, the dead man's rival in love. When they pulled up to the curb outside Weidman's home, the house was dark. As one of the detectives rang the doorbell to rouse the doctor, the other decided to look around the property. When he opened the lid on the garbage can at the curb, he saw a yellow plastic shopping bag lying on top. After putting on gloves, he lifted the bag and a .38 revolver fell out.

When Dr. Weidman finally made it to the door, he was dressed in robe and slippers and seemingly barely awake.

The dentist soon found himself handcuffed and sitting in the back of an unmarked police car.

The two detectives assigned to the case were Dave Andrews and Diego Ramirez. Andrews was about forty, with a round belly and a wide face. I knew him some from working other bail skips; he was a good cop who always showed sympathy toward the victims' families.

I had known Diego since I was a kid. He and my older sister went to their senior prom together, and I was still friends with his brother.

I hung out with them in the squad room that night and listened in as they discussed the case. Neither man seemed convinced of Dr. Weidman's guilt. They both thought that finding the gun in the garbage can was a little too convenient. And as for Bobbi Reed, well, they were just waiting to see what the surveillance tapes revealed.

~

It was nearly noon the next day when the ballistic results came back. The gun that murdered Lucinda was the same gun that murdered her husband, and his Lolita.

Dr. Weidman hadn't been charged with murder yet but was being held for questioning. He vehemently denied his guilt and pointed out to the detectives that he had already been cleared of Lucinda's murder. At the time she was killed, he had been at a dental convention in Miami.

When the detectives asked the doctor for the name of his accomplice, he demanded to see his lawyer.

Meanwhile, the hospital security video seemed to back-up Bobbi Reed. Although, surveillance was incomplete, because the three cameras around the loading dock area weren't working. In addition, there was a twenty-six-minute gap where she was out of camera view; she explained this by saying that at the time, she was outside on the loading dock, smoking, a definite no-no for someone fighting liver cancer.

I was going to miss my run with Becca, so I gave her a call and filled her in on what was happening.

"So, when do I get to meet this Gary?"

"Whoa, Mom, it's too soon for that. We haven't even had a real date yet."

"Okay, but I want to meet him if it goes past a third date."

"It's a deal."

"Now, what about these murders, do you think the doctor did it?"

"No, and despite what Gary believes, I can't buy Bobbi Reed as a triple murderer."

"Whoever did it would have to of known about the girl, Sarah? Who knew about her besides Bobbi Reed?"

I thought about that, and when the answer came to me, I nearly dropped my phone.

~

Rachel Reed looked every bit the innocent. Her big blue eyes widened as I entered the trailer with the two homicide detectives, Dave Andrews and Diego Ramirez. Accompanying us were four police officers and a police psychiatrist named Debra Walker. Two of the officers wore their standard dark blue uniforms, but the other two were dressed in gray coveralls.

Bobbi Reed spread her arms wide. "I figured you'd be by sooner or later. Go ahead, search all you want. I didn't kill anybody, and I've got nothing to hide."

Diego handed her the warrants. "These officers will

search, and while they do that, ma'am, would you mind if we sat and talked?"

"Talked about what?"

Rachel's eyes followed the two officers in coveralls as they went outside.

"Why are those two leaving?"

"Oh, they're not leaving," Diego said. "They'll be searching outside, even crawling under the motor home."

Rachel sent him a shaky smile and sat on the couch beside her mother.

As we all settled in, Detective Andrews took out a notebook and read from it.

"Mrs. Reed, did you know that Dr. Weidman's home is only a short drive from the hospital?"

"Yes, I mean, Lucinda took us there to meet him once, when things got serious between them."

"Do you own a firearm, ma'am?"

"Yes, I have a gun; it's an old .38 my husband bought at a gun show years ago. It's in a shoebox at the back of my closet."

Detective Andrews hollered, "Miller?" and one of the officers stuck his head out of the bedroom.

"Yes sir?"

"Have you guys come across a gun in a shoebox, probably in the closet?"

"We found a shoebox, but there were only a few loose shells rolling around in it, no gun."

"Thank you," Andrews said, and the cop went back to searching.

Bobbi Reed sat with an open mouth. "My gun is gone?"

One of the cops in coveralls came inside carrying a duffel bag. He spoke to Diego.

"We found this in the trunk of that rusted Beetle."

Diego put on a pair of latex gloves, then he opened the bag and began to empty it of its contents. He took out toys, hair ribbons with ponies on them, ticket stubs from concerts that happened years ago, and preteen-sized skirts and tops that, if worn, would be very revealing. As he dug deeper into the bag, he came across a nightie that was nothing short of X-rated. It was scarlet red and void of material in the most interesting places.

"Mrs. Reed, do you recognize any of these articles, ma'am?"

Bobbi Reed shook her head as she stared over at her daughter. "No, I've never seen them before."

When Rachel spoke, it was almost a whisper. "They're mine, put them back."

Diego continued to search. He found photos in an outside pocket of the duffel bag. I could tell from the look on his face that our worst fears had been confirmed. He stood and looked through them slowly, as Detective Andrews, and Debra Walker, the police psychiatrist, peered over his shoulder.

Diego then looked over at me and mouthed two words. "It's bad."

I later learned that they were all photos of Rachel. In the earliest of the pictures, Rachel couldn't have been more than five. In the latest, she looked as she did now. But there were other photos of the years in between, and in each photo, she was nude.

Debra Walker beckoned for Bobbi to join them, and Diego went through the photos again.

Bobbi viewed the evidence of her daughter's molestation, as tears fell from her eyes.

"Oh God, oh Vinnie you miserable prick, not my baby too, not my baby."

Rachel looked at the floor as she spoke. "I wasn't

molested; Vincent loved me. He always loved me, not Lucinda, and that slut Sarah was nothing to him. He loved me, me! He only stayed with Lucinda all those years because it made it possible for us to be together, and I-I loved him too."

"If you loved him, then why did you murder him?" Diego asked.

Bobbi turned away from the obscene photos and settled back onto the sofa.

"What... what did you say?"

"Your daughter killed Vincent Caine and Sarah Miller, and I'm sorry to tell you this, ma'am, but she also killed her sister. If I had to guess, I'd say it was because Lucinda found these photos and threatened to have Vincent arrested. Rachel murdered Caine and Sarah Miller out of jealousy."

Bobbi turned her head and stared at Rachel as if she were looking at a deformed stranger. Afterwards, she fell back against the couch in a near faint.

Debra Walker went to Bobbi and took her pulse. "Will someone please get her a glass of water?"

I walked toward the kitchen area to grab a bottle of water from the refrigerator. As I moved past her, I stared at Rachel Reed. I was certain she was a murderer three times over, but those big blue eyes and perfectly dimpled cheeks still made her look angelic.

As Bobbi took the water from me, she reached for her purse, then removed a pill bottle.

"My medicine," she said, "Let me take my medicine and then we'll talk."

After she had swallowed the pills, she placed a hand lovingly against Rachel's cheek.

"I love you, baby; everything is going to be okay."

Rachel sent her a weak smile.

Afterward, Bobbi stared at Diego. "I confess. I killed my daughter, Vincent, and that Sarah girl. I killed them all and my Rachel had nothing to do with it."

Diego sighed. "Mrs. Reed, I appreciate the fact that you want to protect your daughter. However, it's not possible for you to have killed Vincent Caine and to have also planted the murder weapon at Dr. Weidman's home. We checked, and you just wouldn't have had enough time. Plus, you didn't even have a vehicle; your daughter drops you off at night and picks you up in the morning, which gave her plenty of time in between to commit the crimes."

"The bakery delivers to the hospital cafeteria every night, and the driver always talks a while with the girl on the night shift. While he was inside, I stole his van and committed the murders."

"We talked to the driver; in fact, he confirms that you were smoking out at the loading dock during the time you were away from the cameras."

"He's lying. I did it. I used his delivery van, caught every light green, and made it back before I was missed."

Detective Andrews shook his head. "No ma'am, I'm afraid not." He then stared down at Rachel. "Miss Reed, please come with us to the station; I think we need to talk."

Bobbi Reed slumped back on the couch. "Are you people deaf? I said that I confess to everything. I killed my daughter, I killed Vinnie and I killed Sarah Miller."

"Sorry ma'am, but I just ain't buyin' it," Andrews said. "I think you would do anything to protect your daughter."

Bobbi smiled a lazy smile. "It's a death bed confession; you have to believe it."

"I know about your health problems, and I'm sorry about that, but you're still a ways from passing on."

"Detective, did you know that I've worked at the same hospital for over twenty years?"

"No, ma'am."

"It's true, and I could have worked on any shift I wanted, so why do you think I chose to switch to the night shift three weeks ago?"

"Yes, why would you do that?" Diego said, as he moved closer to her.

We all waited to hear the answer, but Bobbi seemed to be slipping off to sleep; then, with a jerk, she came back.

"I worked the night shift... because it's much easier then... to steal from the pharmacy, and I never had any intention of dying while suffering." She looked over at Rachel. "I love you so much, baby. Put... put all this behind you and have a good life." Then, Bobbi's eyes rolled back, and her head lolled over.

"Pharmacy?" I said. "Oh God, what she swallowed, that wasn't medicine; it was poison!"

Andrews cursed, then called for an ambulance, as Dr. Walker worked on reviving Bobbi.

Within the hour, Bobbi Reed was pronounced dead.

~

TWO WEEKS LATER, GARY AND I WERE HAVING SUNDAY brunch at a little bistro in Dallas.

"So, Rachel Reed just walks away, huh?"

Gary nodded. "The DA says that Bobbi Reed's confession is good enough for her, and besides, she's in a tight race. If they tried Rachel and she walked, it could tank the DA's bid for reelection."

"Rachel Reed murdered those people, not Bobbi," I said.

"Rachel's lawyer, Sam Coulton, he had his investigators do a reenactment of Vinnie's murder, and yes, if every light were green and Bobbi Reed drove like an absolute madwoman, she would have had just enough time to commit the murders and plant the gun at the doctor's."

"Where is Rachel now?"

"Off to live with relatives of her late father, at least until she turns eighteen."

"That girl, as innocent as she appears, is a murderer."

"I agree, but the law says different," Gary said, and then he leaned across the table and kissed me. "No more shop talk, besides, I want to ask you a question."

"Ask away."

"I'm going out to the ranch next weekend; would you like to come along?"

"Absolutely, I can't wait to see it."

"We'd ah, we'd be staying all weekend, overnight, you know?"

I grinned. "I look forward to it."

Gary smiled back and took my hand. "Blue Steele, what a tough name for such a sweet woman."

"The people I catch don't think I'm sweet."

"I don't know; I think you may have captured me."

"Really? Well then, what's the bounty?"

Gary sighed. "The slightly used heart of a lonely man."

I gave his hand a squeeze. "I'll take it."

PART TWO

GOING HOME

CHAPTER 7

I leaned back in the passenger seat of the pickup truck as we headed toward hell, I mean home.

I glanced over at Gary and shook my head. A boyfriend, I had an actual boyfriend, and unlike the last few, I liked this one. Now don't get me wrong, I liked all my boyfriends, at first.

But sooner or later, usually sooner, one of us, all right, *I*, would get bored, or feel penned in, or just become afraid of being tied down to someone forever. So far, I've felt none of that with Gary.

A defense lawyer? How did I wind up dating a defense lawyer? I asked myself. And then Gary turned his head and smiled that sexy smile at me and I knew how I wound up dating him.

The man was a hunk.

"Blue?"

I snapped out of my woolgathering. "Huh?"

"You're not nervous, are you?"

"About you meeting my family? No, but like I said earlier—"

"I know, you said that your mother has no filter on her mouth, that whatever she thinks, she says."

"Well, it's true, and my sister is—"

"Overly friendly and highly competitive."

"No, my sister is a spoiled brat who can't stand it when I have something she doesn't, including men. I could give you the names of at least three boyfriends she's stolen away from me over the years."

"Well, don't worry; no matter how many times I sleep with her, I'll always come back to you."

"What?"

"Blue, it was a joke, calm down."

I pointed to the shoulder of the road. "Pull over, please?"

Gary drove his pickup over to the side of the road and shut off the engine. Afterward, he turned in his seat and looked at me expectantly.

"Blue?"

"I don't want to lose you, Gary. I know we've only been dating for a few weeks, but my family, all kidding aside, they can be difficult. I don't want them to scare you off."

"Blue, baby, I can handle your mom and your sister, believe me. I'm only tagging along because I couldn't stand the thought of being without you for three days."

I kissed him. "It's no wonder you win most of your cases; you always know the right thing to say."

Gary stared at me with a question on his lips, but then stayed silent.

"What? What were you going to say?"

"I have a confession to make."

"Yes?"

"I went on the internet last night and researched your dad. It's just that you never talk about him and now that we're going to see your family, I thought that—"

"It's okay," I said, cutting him off. "I find it difficult to talk about him; it always brings back bad memories."

"I can understand that, I mean the not knowing, it must be hard."

"I should have told you, especially now, in fact, I'm only going home because it's his birthday; it's become a tradition. My mother insists that we gather around his birthday."

"It makes sense to me, as a way to honor him, and you know what?"

"What?"

Gary took my hand. "This year you don't have to face it alone."

"Thank you."

"For what?"

"Just thank you."

"Well, you're welcome," Gary said, and then he pulled back onto the road.

~

My daddy, the original Blue Steele, was a Texas Ranger, as was his daddy, and his daddy, and his daddy.

When I was seventeen, my father went missing while investigating a serial killer.

Daddy was convinced that one man had been killing across the country for over five decades without being detected. The means he used to kill, as well as the victims he chose, were so varied, that the experts attributed the deaths to multiple persons.

To this day, no one knows what became of my father, and his theory of a "Herd Thinner" as it came to be called, was greatly discounted by experts. My father had many friends, Texas Ranger Deke Thomas, was among them. They had all searched for clues to my father's whereabouts and for proof that the man he'd pursued wasn't just a figment of his imagination.

Now, over ten years later, Daddy is listed as missing, presumed dead, and the man he sought, his "Herd Thinner", if he existed, would likely be well into his eighties, or dead.

∼

GARY TURNED OFF THE HIGHWAY AND HEADED DOWN THE gravel road that led to my family home.

We were in Landsville, Texas. Landsville was a small town just outside of Garland, where my father had been stationed with the Texas Rangers' Company B Headquarters.

The town was mostly farm and ranch land with a small downtown area that now boasted its own McDonald's, and the movie theater had recently begun opening seven days a week. It was a great town to grow up in, and despite the angst of family tension, I was glad to be home.

Gary drove past the barn and parked in front of the garage. Before he could even turn off the engine, my mama and sister came out to greet us.

My sister Jenny and I had both gotten our long dark hair from our mama, only now, Mama's hair was a luminescent white that hung about her smiling face like a snowy mane. Her blue eyes sent me a twinkle and then immediately began assessing Gary.

My sister was also staring at Gary, while smiling a predatory grin. My sister is two years older than I am, but other than her blue eyes, we look like twins. When she had given Gary the once over, she turned her gaze on me and smiled.

"Welcome home, Blue, and who's the hunk?" Jenny said.

I ignored her and gave my mama a hug. Although coming home was always stressful, I loved my mama to death and suddenly realized how much I had missed her.

"Hey, Mama, how you been?"

She smiled at me as she caressed my cheek. "I've been good, girl, but look at how skinny you are. Well, I'll fix that; I'll put five pounds on you before you leave." And then she looked at Gary. "This must be Gary; he's a little old for you, ain't he? How old are you, mister?"

Gary didn't even blink. "I'm forty."

"Forty? Well hell, that's pushin' the envelope, but you are a sexy devil, I'll give you that."

"Are you flirting with me, ma'am?"

"Am I...?" Mama said, and then she laughed. "No, son, I'm too old for that nonsense. Hell, if I want a man, I just tell him so."

Gary smiled. "A plainspoken woman, I like that."

"How do you feel about my daughter?"

"I like her a great deal."

"In the sack or out of it?"

"Both," Gary said, without the trace of a blush, although I could feel my cheeks redden.

"You treat her good out of the sack and she'll treat you good in it; we Steele women know how to take care of a man."

Jenny sidled up against Gary then. "All us Steele women know how to treat a man right. Hi, I'm Jenny."

"It's nice to meet both of you ladies, but why don't we go inside? I don't know about Blue, but I could use a drink of water."

"Or something stronger," I mumbled.

Just as we reached the top of the porch steps, a car

traveled up the long driveway and came to a sliding halt beside Gary's truck. It was the sheriff's car, behind it, followed a patrol car.

County Sheriff Matt Walker had been sheriff for as long as I could remember, although he was only in his early fifties. He had taken the job over from his father, Joe Walker, who had died from cancer. Joe Walker had been a legend in these parts, and even had a street in town named after him.

Matt Walker was a tall, thin man with a no-nonsense face and short blond hair turning gray. After exiting his cruiser, he came over to us, with one of the deputies following behind. The other deputy, a boy I grew up with named Billy Joe Tently, looked about the property.

The sheriff tipped his hat at my mother. "Howdy, Maggie." Next, he spotted me and broke out in a smile. "Well I'll be, little Blue, how you doin' there, girl?"

I walked over and kissed him on the cheek. "I'm fine, Sheriff, and it's good to see you again, but hey, what brings you out here?"

Sheriff Matt ducked his head and sighed. "I'm sorry to say it's official business," he said, and stared at Jenny. "Miss Steele, do you know a man by the name of Thomas Hayes?"

Jenny grinned. "Tommy? Yes, he's my boyfriend."

"When was the last time you saw him?"

"Last night, we had dinner in Garland and... then we went back to his place."

"And what time did you leave?"

Jenny's eyes looked up, as she thought about it. "I guess it was around two a.m."

Mama snorted. "Two a.m.? The boy's got more stamina than I would have given him credit for."

Jenny frowned at her. "We fell asleep while watching a movie, Mama. Sheriff, what's this about?"

"I'm sorry to tell you this, Jenny, but Tommy Hayes is dead."

Jenny shook her head violently. "What?"

"Yes, he was stabbed through the heart; the coroner places the time of death at around two a.m."

"Tommy, dead? Wait... you think I killed him?"

"I don't think anything yet," Sheriff Matt said.

Billy Joe called over from the side of the barn; he was standing beside Jenny's car, an old green Chevy Impala.

"We got a bloody knife here on the passenger seat, Sheriff."

"What knife?" Jenny said. "There's no knife in my car."

The sheriff's phone beeped, and he checked it. After giving it a perturbed look, he held it up so that we could all look at it. Billy Joe must have taken a photo of the car and sent it to him. The picture showed the inside of Jenny's car, lying on the passenger seat was a knife that looked like a switchblade; it was covered in blood.

The sheriff called over to his deputy. "Billy Joe, stay with the car while we head back to town. I'm going to see about getting a warrant. I want everything by the book on this one. And oh yeah, stop sending me stuff on the damn phone. There's nothing wrong with my legs, I could have just walked over there and looked in. Miss Jenny, I need you to come to the station with me so we can talk, and uh, you might want to have a lawyer handy."

I spoke to him. "There's more, isn't there, Sheriff? I can tell by the look on your face."

"We have witnesses, Blue, and that's all I'm gonna say for now."

Gary stepped forward. "Hello, Sheriff, my name is

Gary Dent. I'm Blue's boyfriend and now... I guess I'm also Jenny's attorney."

"All right, then why don't you follow us back into town. Jenny, you'll be riding with me."

The other deputy took out a set of handcuffs and Jenny blanched. The sheriff raised a hand and spoke up.

"Put those cuffs away, Bob, there's no need for them, right, Jenny?"

"Yes," Jenny said. She was crying and looked devastated by the loss of her boyfriend, and the possibility that she might be blamed for his murder.

Sheriff Matt offered his arm and then he escorted Jenny to his car.

With Mama sitting in the back seat of Gary's pickup, we followed the police cars out to the highway.

"Mr. Gary?" Mama said.

Gary looked at her in the rearview mirror.

"Yes, ma'am?"

"Guilty or not, you get my girl free, you hear me?"

"Guilty or not, yes, ma'am."

"Well, all right then," Mama said, and off we went to the police station.

CHAPTER 8

According to Mama, Jenny had been dating Tommy Hayes for over six months, a record for my sister.

Tommy had been a reporter, based out of Dallas, and as far as Mama knew, he never had a problem with anyone.

Gary followed the sheriff and Jenny into an interrogation room when we arrived at the local police station.

The station was in a massive old building that also housed the courthouse and licensing bureaus. Despite its gray stone exterior, the inside was modern, thanks to a renovation three years earlier.

Mama and I sat for hours on a wooden bench while sipping on vending machine coffee. After what seemed like forever, Gary walked over and sat beside us.

"They're booking her on suspicion of murder, chiefly because of the knife found in her car. DNA results on the blood aren't in yet of course, but the blood type matches the victim, Tommy Hayes."

"What's Jenny's story?" I said.

"She says he was fine when she left him. Tommy

walked her out to her car, and she drove off. She has no idea how the knife got into her car. And oh, they searched the house and removed all of Jenny's clothes, plus her car. She'll be arraigned in the morning. If they find any more evidence, they may up the charge to murder."

"Mama," I said. "Does Jenny ever lock her car?"

"No, there's no need, and you're thinking that somebody planted that knife, aren't you?"

"Yes, Jenny wouldn't kill anybody, and if she did, she'd be smart enough to get rid of the murder weapon."

"That's what I think too," said a voice from the doorway. We all looked up to see Sheriff Matt enter the room.

Mama walked over to him. "If you think my girl is innocent, then why are you keeping her here?"

"Maggie, I have to go where the evidence takes me, despite how I feel."

"Sheriff," I said. "You said there were witnesses, who are they?"

"It's Doc Monroe and Emma Cole."

Mama hung her head. "Oh, Lordy."

"What am I missing?" Gary said. "I take it that Doc Monroe is a doctor of some kind, but who is Emma Cole?"

I answered him. "Doc Monroe isn't a doctor, he's *the* doctor. He's about eighty, highly respected, and he must have delivered nearly every baby in this town, including me and Jenny."

"And Emma Cole?"

"She's the mayor, and her late husband's family founded the town."

Gary sighed. "I suppose they'd have no reason to lie."

"Doc said he saw Jenny and Tommy fighting," the sheriff said. "Doc said it was loud enough to wake him up. His house is directly across from the Martin place; Tommy rents the apartment over the Martin's garage."

"What about the Martins?" I said. "If a fight were loud enough to wake Doc, then it would have woken them up too. What do they say?"

"No one was home, they're on vacation."

"And Emma Cole, what's her story? Why would the mayor be up at two a.m.?"

"Emma suffers from insomnia. When she can't sleep, she goes out for a drive. She says she saw Jenny at a stop light by the convenience store on Main Street. Emma said that Jenny had blood on her face and wouldn't look at her. When the light changed, Jenny sped off."

"What's Jenny say about all this?" I said.

"She denies everything, says there was never a fight, no knife and no blood, says she doesn't know why Doc and the mayor would say what they're saying."

Mama shook her head slightly.

"None of this makes sense."

"Well, it could," Sheriff Matt said.

Mama stared at him. "How's that?"

"Maybe, just maybe Jenny suffered a break of some kind, a mental break. If she murdered Tommy in a fit of rage or jealousy, she may have blocked it from her mind."

"That's crazy!" Mama shouted.

"Crazier than Doc and the mayor making up stories to frame her? Why would they lie, Maggie?" the sheriff said.

"I don't know," Mama said quietly.

I didn't know either, but if they were lying, I was going to find out why.

CHAPTER 9

Mama and I were allowed to visit with Jenny in a small, windowless room. I was surprised to see her dressed in what looked like a set of orange hospital scrubs, but then I realized that they would have taken her clothes for processing.

Jenny sent us a weak smile as we settled across from her at a gray metal table.

"I didn't do it," she said.

"Tell us what you remember about last night," I said. "Did anything out of the ordinary happen? Was Tommy worried about anything, maybe afraid of something?"

"No he was in a very good mood. He said the story he was working on was about to break open."

"What story?"

"I don't know, but Tommy wasn't a crime reporter or anything, he wrote for the Lifestyle section, plus the occasional human-interest story."

"That doesn't sound like an area where a story could 'break open'; maybe he was working on something more serious."

Jenny began to cry, and Mama reached over and held her hand.

"What is it, baby?"

"Tommy, I was falling in love with him, Mama. Goddamn whoever killed him; I hope they rot in hell."

"First, we have to figure out who that is," I said. "What do you remember about your ride home?"

"It was quiet; I didn't see another car until I reached the highway. I don't know why Doc would say Tommy and I fought. And the mayor, she was nowhere in sight, but why would they lie? I don't understand why they would lie about me."

I stared at Jenny. "Hey, Jen, think hard before you answer me, but are you certain you remember the ride home?"

Jenny screwed up her face in thought. "Yes, I remember Tommy kissing me goodbye. I remember sitting at that damn long light on Maple Street, and then heading up the ramp and merging onto the high—"

"Maple Street? You took Maple Street home, not Main Street?"

"Yeah, I know it's a little longer drive, but it puts you up farther along the highway, why?"

"The mayor claims she saw you on Main Street, not Maple."

"Well then, she's definitely lying. Even if I somehow missed seeing her, she couldn't have seen me on Main Street; I was never there."

"I need to go have a talk with Doc and the mayor," I said.

Billy Joe Tently stuck his head in the room. He was a muscular man of average height with a toothy grin. He was the youngest of seven brothers and his father had been my math teacher in high school. One thing about growing up in a small town is that you know just about everyone's history.

"Time's up, ladies, but you'll be able to see her again in the morning."

I smiled. "Okay Billy Joe, but just give us a second, huh?"

He smiled back. "Sure thing, Blue; I'll be right down the hall." and then he took out his phone and fiddled with it.

After Billy Joe left, I spoke to Jenny.

"Hey, big sis, we're gonna get you out of here, you got that?"

"How?"

I stood up. "Don't you worry about how, just believe me when I say it's gonna get done."

Jenny and Mama stared up at me with their mouths open.

"What?"

Mama grinned. "Damn girl, for just a second there, it sounded like your daddy was talkin'"

~

Gary and I got to Doc's house just as the last patient of the day was leaving. Doc was semi-retired, but still saw the occasional patient; usually they were old friends of his.

As I rang the doorbell, a new BMW parked at the curb, it was Mayor Cole. Emma Cole had to be nearing eighty, but thanks to plastic surgery, she could pass for sixty. She left the car and walked over to us.

"Blue, dear, I heard you were back in town, I'm so sorry that it had to be under such horrible circumstances."

"Hello, Mayor, are you certain it was my sister you saw last night?"

Her face darkened. "I don't want to talk about that; it's a police matter."

"A police matter? Mayor, this is my sister's future we're talking about."

The door opened and Doc Monroe stood there staring at us.

"Come on in, Emma, and Blue, I have nothing to say to you, like Emma said, it's police business."

"Doc, what the hell is going on? Why won't you talk to me?"

The mayor brushed past me and entered the house, then, she swiveled about and pointed a finger at me.

"Leave Blue, or we'll call the sheriff and he'll make you leave."

And then the door shut in my face.

Gary looked at me and grinned. "I see it's true what they say about small town folk being friendly."

"It's not funny. The mayor's always been a bit of a cold fish, but Doc? Doc Monroe is one of the friendliest people I know."

"Not anymore," Gary said. "And I'll tell you something else."

"What?"

"He wasn't just rude, he looked scared."

∽

WE LEFT DOC'S AND DROVE INTO DALLAS.

After a short wait, Gary and I spoke to Ray Kurtz. Kurtz was Tommy Hayes' editor. We talked with him in a small break area behind the newsroom. The clickety-click of numerous people typing at once, even on modern keyboards, still carried into the room.

"I'm just sick about Tommy, Miss Steele, but I have no idea what story he could have been working on. Tommy worked the Lifestyle section mainly, with now and then, a human-interest story."

"What sort of human-interest stories?"

"Oh, you know, like when a lost child is found safe, or a bum on skid row inherits a fortune, stuff like that. I believe the last story he did was about a guy celebrating his 100th birthday at the nursing home." Kurtz suddenly looked thoughtful. "You know, come to think of it, Tommy did tell me that something interesting happened at the home that day. When I asked him what it was, he told me he'd get back to me after he checked some things out."

"How long ago was this?"

"Two days ago, the name of the nursing home is Avalon Health; it's over on Burgoyne Avenue."

∽

We grabbed a quick bite at a diner, while on our way over to the home.

While Gary checked in with his office, I gave my best friend, Becca, a call.

"Wow Blue, that doesn't sound like Doc at all."

"I know, I think he's afraid of something, or somebody."

"Well girl, you tell Jenny that I said to hang in there, the truth will come out eventually."

"Oh, it'll come out all right, even if I have to drag it out by its tail."

Becca laughed, then asked me a question. "How's Gary getting along with your mama?"

"Great, she didn't faze him in the least."

"I think you've got a good one there, Blue, you know?"

I leaned away from the table and lowered my voice.

"Yeah, I know, but it's still early, I mean we've only been together for a few weeks."

"If it counts any, I vote you hang on to him."

"It counts, and I'll keep that in mind."

~

THE ADMINISTRATOR OF THE NURSING HOME WAS A MIDDLE-aged woman with her hair in a severe bun. She was a good-looking woman, but her demeanor told you that she was one tough cookie. At first, she seemed reluctant to let us talk with the staff, but after Gary poured on the charm, she was ready to give us a tour.

I left Gary alone with her to keep her busy, while I talked with the caregiver who had shown Tommy around. Her name was LaShonda Miller. She had a gold cross pinned to her sweater.

"It was Mr. Geary who had the 100th birthday, but honestly, Mr. Hayes seemed more interested in Mr. Blaine; he talked to him for hours that day."

"Who's Mr. Blaine?"

"Andrew Blaine, he's 88 and suffering from Alzheimer's, he's in the early stages though, so he has good days now and then. It helped him find Jesus, that's one good thing that came out of it."

"Is today a good day or a bad day?"

LaShonda smiled. "Let's find out."

~

ANDREW BLAINE WAS LYING IN BED WEARING A ROBE. IN A corner of the room, a TV was playing religious programming. And thankfully, he was having a good day mentally.

"Tommy Hayes, Lord yes, I remember him, good boy. And I swear he's the spittin' image of my kid brother Albert, only Albert died years ago, in Korea."

I pulled a chair close to the bed and sat. "What did you two talk about, sir?"

"Not to be disrespectful, ma'am, but that's between me and Tommy. But don't worry, once he writes his story, the whole world will know."

I told him about Tommy then, and he seemed to shrink inside himself. A moment later, he mumbled something.

"I'm sorry sir, I couldn't hear you; what did you say?"

He lifted his head and stared at me with young blue eyes trapped in an ancient face.

"I said the bastards killed him."

"What bastards?"

Blaine reached over to his bedside table and grabbed a bible. "Their day of reckoning has come. Listen up, missy; I'm about to tell you a story."

And he sure did. When he was done, I was certain I knew who killed Tommy Hayes, and why.

CHAPTER 10

We arrived back in Landsville late in the evening, then Gary and I spent the night on our laptops doing research.

Mama got up early as usual and made us breakfast. Over coffee, I filled her in.

"That son of a bitch! I should get your daddy's old shotgun and put him in the ground."

"Whoa Mama, we've no proof; it's just a theory at this point. But once I confront him, we'll know if he's guilty or not."

"Your sister is being arraigned this morning at nine o'clock; we'll talk to him then."

I shook my head. "*I'll* talk to him then. This could be dangerous, and if it is, I don't want you anywhere around."

"I know you're damn near as tough as your daddy, girl, but get some help, don't face him alone."

"I've already thought of that, and I'm waiting for a call back from the sheriff's department."

∼

We got to the municipal building at half past eight.

Sheriff Matt met me in an unoccupied courtroom, and I repeated Andrew Blaine's story to him. When I was finished, he leaned back on the wooden railing of the witness box.

"Doc and the mayor, bank robbers?"

"Actually, it was an armored car. The heist took place just outside of El Paso, in 1953."

"And this Blaine, he claims to be one of the gang that Doc and Emma were a part of?"

"Yes, he and another man, it was the other man that planned the heist. Andrew Blaine was Emma Cole's boyfriend, of course, back then she was Emma Jameson. Emma, Doc, Blaine, and another man robbed over two hundred thousand dollars that day; they also killed the three guards inside the truck."

"This fourth perp, any idea who he was?"

"Yes, Blaine says he was the brains behind the heist, and also the reason it worked so well."

"How do you mean?"

"The other man was a deputy sheriff; he flagged down the armored car by using his siren. When the driver lowered the window to talk to him, he shot him in the face. After that, Doc and Emma blocked the front, and with the patrol car blocking the rear, the remaining guards had nowhere to go."

Sheriff Matt got off the railing and stood up straight. "And you say this happened in El Paso?"

"Yes, your father, Sheriff Joe, he was from El Paso, wasn't he?"

The sheriff let loose a heavy sigh. "Goddamn it, Blue, why couldn't you just let it go? Your sister could have pleaded diminished capacity and been out in five years."

"And what about Tommy, Sheriff, will Tommy be back in five years?"

"I hated doing that, I really did, but the boy left me no choice. He had no clue who I was. He came and told me Blaine's story in the hope that I would help him identify the deputy from El Paso. Blaine couldn't remember his last name, only that his first name was Joe."

"You knew all this before he came to you, didn't you?"

"Yeah, my daddy confessed to me when he was dying. I told him it didn't make a bit of difference; every man does good and evil. A few years after that heist, daddy met my mama and stopped drinking; from that day forward, he did nothing but good. I'll be damned if I'll let anybody drag his name through the mud, anybody, Blue."

"So, what are you going to do, Sheriff, kill me? It won't do any good, other people know about Andrew Blaine."

"Blaine's just a silly old coot with Alzheimer's, besides, Doc is on his way there now to... ease him to the other side. As for you, I guess I'll say that you were attempting to break your sister out."

"I'm not Tommy, Sheriff. I have a gun and I know how to use it."

"Little Blue, named after her daddy, are you as fast with a gun as he was? Well, I guess we'll find out."

"No we won't, Sheriff," said a voice from behind him.

It was Deputy Billy Joe Tently, I had told him my suspicions about the sheriff, and he reluctantly agreed to hide himself beneath the judge's bench and listen in. Now, he stood behind his boss with his weapon drawn.

"Billy Joe, put down that gun."

Billy Joe shook his head. "Afraid not. Now, take out your weapon slowly and lay it on the witness seat there."

The sheriff did as he was told and then smiled. "This

don't matter none, once Doc takes care of Blaine, it will all just be hearsay."

Billy Joe smiled his big toothy grin. "No sir, we got you on film." He reached over and grabbed his phone off the bench. "And not only was it filming, but it also downloaded to my computer at home."

The sheriff made a pained expression. "You and that goddamn phone, Billy Joe."

As Billy Joe led the sheriff away, I whipped out my own phone and called the nursing home. It took a minute, but I got them to understand the threat to them. They assured me that Mr. Blaine was safe, and that they were alerting security and calling the Dallas P.D.

I walked out of the courtroom and found Gary and Mama smiling at me.

Mama walked over and placed a hand on my cheek. "You done good, girl."

"Thank you, Mama."

"Mr. Gary?"

"Yes, ma'am?"

"Let's go get my other girl free like you promised me."

Gary offered her his arm. "Yes, ma'am."

"Well, all right then," Mama said, and off we went to get Jenny.

PART THREE

CALL ME RAMÓN

CHAPTER 11

I was at the Lone Star Mall.

Earlier, I had eaten lunch in the food court with Becca and her oldest daughter, Amy, who was eight years old.

Becca and Amy were browsing about the mall, while I sat in a chair at the salon getting ready to have my hair dried and my feet pedicured. It was Spoil Blue Day, a day I tried to celebrate at least twice a year.

I had a full schedule planned. After sleeping sinfully late, I drove to the mall and met Becca for lunch. After the salon, I planned to go home and veg out in front of the TV, and later, after a junk food dinner, I would indulge in ice cream, mint chocolate chip.

Gary was out of town on business and wouldn't be back for two days, so it was a perfect time to just sit back and relax. Of course, life had other plans.

The stylist was just about to place the dryer over my head when I heard the gunshots. I, along with the others in the shop, ran to the salon's front windows and looked out at the interior of the mall. We were on the ground floor of the three-story building, and in the middle of our section, there was a coin fountain. Past the stone fountain, on the other side of the mall, was a bank.

As we watched, three armed men in suits ran out of the bank and headed for the exit, the one in the lead was dragging a child along; the child was Amy.

I ran back to my pocketbook and grabbed my gun, a snub-nosed .38. As I did so, I shouted to the shop owner.

"Gloria, call 911, tell them that four men just robbed the bank, shots fired, hostage taken."

"I only saw three."

"There's a driver outside; trust me, they're not walking."

On my way out the door, I grabbed a scrunchie and tied my wet hair back in a ponytail.

As my bare feet slapped against the floor tiles, I maneuvered around groups of huddled shoppers and thumbed back the hammer on my gun.

When I heard more shots ring out, I came to a sliding halt in front of the bank, then watched as the robbers banged open the exit doors. On the floor behind them were two bodies, a man and a woman, both mall security.

I raced toward the doors and made it outside just as the last robber was twenty feet from the getaway car. He was a behemoth and weighed three-hundred and fifty if he was a pound. It was no wonder he was last to reach the car.

"Stop!" I called.

The man turned toward me with an Uzi in his right hand. I shot at him four times while still running. The first three shots missed high, but the fourth one took a chunk of his head off in a spray of blood and brains. As he fell, he spun toward his own vehicle and the gun in his hand began to chatter.

The man sitting in the passenger seat ducked in time, but the driver wasn't as lucky. As he bent forward to avoid the errant shots, his seat belt held him in place, and multiple slugs caused him to dance in his seat. As the gun fell toward the ground along with its owner, it blew apart the right rear tire and etched a line of holes into the ground behind the car.

The man in the back seat scrambled out of the car with Amy and a black satchel, while his sole remaining companion followed behind.

"Let the girl go!" I shouted.

The man shoved Amy toward the other surviving man, then leaned over the trunk of the car.

As he opened up with his gun, I dived to the ground and rolled beside the dead man. He had fallen on his back when he died; his massive bulk made for a handy shield.

I lay as flat as I could as a dozen shots came my way. Many of them plunked into the corpse and at least one exited in a spray of blood. I was wearing a pair of cut-off jeans and the still warm blood splattered across my legs.

"Stop shootin', you're hittin' Bobby," the other man yelled.

I raised my head, risked a glance, and found that the men were running away. They were dragging Amy along between them. Amy's curly blonde hair floated behind her in the breeze. They were running toward the east end of the parking lot, where the highway was.

I stood to go in pursuit, and that's when I heard my name called.

"Blue?"

It was Becca. She had a lump the size of a golf ball above her left eye and appeared to be on the verge of passing out, even so, I breathed a sigh of relief at the sight of her; until that moment, I didn't know if the robbers had killed her.

"Blue they took Amy… they took Amy."

I locked eyes with her. "I'll get her back; I swear it."

Becca nodded slightly, then sank to the ground in tears.

I ignored my impulse to comfort her and ran after the robbers. As I threaded my way through the parking lot, I came upon shoppers hiding in their cars. Many of them held phones to their ears, undoubtedly calling 9-1-1. While the police would be a blessing, I also prayed that their arrival wouldn't escalate things into a hostage situation. I needed to get Amy away from her abductors before the situation got out of hand.

At the end of the parking lot was a rise of grass, twenty feet high, which took you up to the freeway. As the two men reached the top of the slope, one of them fired a shot in my direction. It blew the windshield out of a car thirty feet away from me. It was a weak one-handed shot and was probably only meant to slow me down.

As I started up the hill, they vanished from sight. I slipped and grunted my way up the grass. The morning dew remained and had made the grass slick; my bare feet only made the going tougher.

I was ten feet from the top when I heard shots, which was followed by screeching as a car came to a sudden stop. I made it to the top of the rise just as the robbers peeled away. They were in a Hummer of all things, a blue one. Its previous owner lay on the side of the road, he was unconscious, with blood running down his face.

The Thursday afternoon traffic was light, and the carjacking had barely slowed down the flow.

I needed a ride. I ran out into the middle lane, gun at the ready and searched for the right vehicle. It came a second later in the form of a black Ford F350.

I fired one shot in the air and then stood sideways with the gun aimed at the speeding pickup. The truck slowed, but as it neared me, it veered to the right and skidded to a sideways stop. A moment later, I found myself face-to-face with the driver. His gun made the .38 I carried look like a popgun.

The man smiled, as he thumbed off the safety on the gun.

"Hey Chica, what's happenin'?"

∼

"There!" I pointed. "The black Hummer in the middle lane."

"I see it," said the man in a calm voice, he was about thirty, swarthy, muscular, and good-looking.

"What's your name?"

"Call me Ramón," he said, with a slight Spanish accent.

"I'm Blue."

"The bounty hunter?"

"You've heard of me?"

"Yes, you once got to a man before I could."

"You're a bounty hunter too?"

He smiled, "Not exactly," and then he looked down at my bloody legs. "There are some wipes in the glove box."

I found the wipes and cleaned up, when I finished, I found Ramón staring at my legs.

"Eyes on the road, we can't lose them."

"Sorry, Chica, but you are a little distracting, you know?"

"I only know that my best friend's daughter is in that Hummer with two crazed gunmen. Help me get her back and I'll pose nude if you want."

A smile formed on Ramón's handsome face. "I may hold you to that."

We drove along, following behind the Hummer, while

always keeping two or three cars between us. If they knew we were following, they didn't show it. They just drove along in the middle lane while keeping with the flow of traffic.

I tapped my fingers on the door. "I can't believe you don't have a phone."

"I hate the damn things, besides, there's no one I want to talk to."

"I need to call the cops."

"So, where's your phone?"

"Back in the beauty parlor, along with my pocketbook, and my boots."

"There's a pair of flip-flops behind your seat, they're better than nothing."

I twisted in my seat and reached back to grab a pair of bright red flip-flops. I put them on even though I didn't like them. I disliked the feeling of having anything between my toes, but as Ramón said, they were better than nothing.

"Why are you helping me?" I asked.

"You said that these bastards took a kid; I hate anyone who messes with kids, plus, there's the money they took."

"That money belongs to the bank."

"Finders keepers, Chica."

Up ahead, the Hummer made a right, turned off the highway, and drove down a dirt road. Ramón pulled over to the shoulder and parked.

"What are you doing? We have to keep them in sight."

"We will, but if we follow too closely, they'll hear us coming."

He was right, but it was hard to sit by and do nothing, a moment later, he turned off the engine.

"Why did you do that?"

"Think about where we are. What's on the other side of these trees?"

We had followed the thieves along highway 31, headed west.

"The Trinity, the Trinity River is back there," I said.

"Correct, so this road must be the only way in or out. From here on in, it looks like we're on foot. If we go driving in there, they'll hear us for sure."

I opened my door. "Let's go."

∾

As we crept along, it occurred to me that I had only one round left in my gun. However, Ramón's hand cannon, a .50 Desert Eagle, held eight rounds.

We walked down the narrow dirt road, staying to either side, so that we didn't make ourselves into one convenient target. As we walked, we listened for any sounds of movement or talking.

We had only gone about a hundred yards when we heard the voices, two of them, arguing.

"She can identify us, Toby. Do you want to spend the rest of your life in Huntsville?"

"Derek, she's just a kid."

We crept closer. Through a break in the trees, I could see the river calmly flowing by, a few steps more and I spotted the two men. The taller of the two had stringy blond hair and a goatee. His gun was out; it was hanging by his side. The other one stood before him, and from where I was, it looked as if Amy was trying to hide behind him.

"Move, Toby, it's gotta be done, so let me do it; we can't stay here all day. That damn Hummer might have GPS tracking and I ain't goin' to be here when the cops find it. Now move!"

The one called Toby was shoved aside, leaving Amy exposed.

"Ramón?"

"I got it," Ramón said, as he sighted down the barrel of his gun.

"Pull that trigger and you're a dead man," said a deep voice from behind us.

We both spun at the sound and, as he turned, Ramón was slammed on the side of the head with a shotgun. He fell limply to the ground. I brought my gun up to fire and the man whipped the shotgun back around and knocked the weapon out of my hand with the barrel.

Pain shot through my arm from my fingertips to my elbow and I wondered if he had just broken my hand.

The other two men came running over with Amy being pulled along. They stared down at us.

The one named Derek glared at me. "It's the bitch from the mall, the one that killed Bobby."

Amy looked over at me with tears in her eyes. "Aunt Blue?"

I smiled at her. "It's okay, baby, Aunt Blue's come to take you home."

A second later, the shotgun rushed toward my face, and everything went black.

CHAPTER 12

I awoke to find my wrists and ankles bound with plastic restraints, while my head was on fire with pain. Beside me, Ramón was still unconscious, and also restrained. Beyond him was Amy, huddled in a corner of the van. Her arms were wrapped around her knees as she hugged herself.

We were in a panel van with a plywood floor and blacked-out side and rear windows. From up front in the cab, I could hear murmured voices.

"Amy," I whispered.

Her eyes grew wide in the ambient light, and she crawled over to me.

"Aunt Blue."

"Hey baby, how you doin'? Those men didn't hurt you any, did they?"

"No, but they're scary."

"I know baby, and I know things look bad right now, but I'll get you back to your mommy as soon as I can, okay?"

She nodded, then winced while staring at me.

"What's wrong?" I said.

She pointed at my face. "Your left eye, it's closed, and kinda purple."

I forced a smile. "I'll be fine in a few days."

Just then, Ramón stirred. "Oohhh, what happened?"

"We got outflanked."

"Oh," Ramón said, and then he smiled at Amy. "Hey there, little one, what's your name?"

"I'm Amy."

"I am Ramón, Amy; and it is very nice to meet you. I would shake your hand, but I'm a little tied up right now."

Amy actually grinned.

Ramón smiled back, and a moment later, the van made a sharp left. Four minutes passed, and then we stopped.

After the passenger doors opened and shut, we heard brief footfalls, then the side door of the van slid open. I had thought that the windows were blacked-out but was now shocked to see that it was nighttime, the only light came from a crescent moon. Ramón and I must have been unconscious for hours. If we had been on the road all that time, then God only knew where they had taken us. The one called Derek yanked first Ramón, and then me out of the van and onto hard packed earth, afterward, he glared in at Amy.

"Toby, why is this little bitch not tied up like the other two?"

The one called Toby walked over. He was a slightly built man with a round, boyish face and a tiny mouth. He spoke to Derek while looking at the ground.

"I didn't need to tie her up; she wasn't going anywhere, Derek."

Derek let out his breath in a huff and climbed in the van to restrain Amy, as the third man moved around to stare down at Ramón and me. He was about six feet tall, like Derek, but he carried an extra twenty pounds of muscle. His hair was short and as black as the night.

I looked about and saw nothing but flat land in all directions, but then to the west, I made out a small rectangle of light that must have been over a mile away. It might have been a lit window in a house, but in the darkness, any surrounding features were lost.

I looked back up, and the third man, the one who had wielded the shotgun, was staring at me. He was gazing down at me in a way that made the lecherous glance Ramón had given me earlier seem like a smile from a favorite uncle.

Ramón had been admiring me; this man was inventorying me. As his tongue crept out and wet his lower lip, I knew he planned to do more than simply get rid of me.

The man stopped his staring and spoke. "Derek, you and Toby take this dude and the kid and drop 'em in the old well out there." The man then reached into a jacket pocket and took out a knife that looked like a switchblade; he held it up. "Use your knife, you still got it?"

"Yeah," Derek said. "But why don't I just shoot 'em?"

The man pointed toward the light in the field, as the knife disappeared back into his pocket.

"The sound of the gun might carry, might not, but we don't need any lookie-loos coming over to butt in, know what I mean?"

Derek nodded, then he glanced at me. "What about her?"

The man smiled down at me. "She'll find her way to the bottom of that well soon enough, but it would be a damn shame to let a piece of ass like this go to waste. She and me, we're gonna spend a little quality time in the van first."

Ramón spat at the man, while shifting his feet beneath him.

"You are a piece of shit! What kind of man rapes women and harms children?"

The man wiped the spittle off his chin, then reared back a foot to kick Ramón. Ramón launched himself at the man. The two of them slammed against the side of the van, before sliding down into the dirt.

Derek pulled Ramón off the other man and began kicking him repeatedly. I screamed at him to stop, while Amy began crying. Finally, the beating ended, and Ramón rolled over to me. He was bleeding from his mouth and his nose. I knew the repeated kicks to his midsection must have caused damage, but when I looked into his eyes, he winked.

A second later, I felt something hard strike my thigh. When I looked down, I saw the knife, and realized that he had taken it from the third man's pocket as they struggled in the dirt.

I shifted over and plucked it from the ground. It took two tries though, because my hand was swollen from being swatted with the shotgun. I had just managed to palm the knife when the third man pulled me up on my feet by yanking on my ponytail. The next thing I knew, I was landing atop the plywood floor of the van.

"Remember, Derek, no guns, stick that pig with your knife until he begs you to stop and then cut his throat."

"My pleasure," Derek said. Then, I heard them moving away, toward the left.

I explored the knife with my thumb and found a button. I was right; it was a switchblade.

The man climbed in the van and turned to slide the door shut. The noise the door created masked the small sound the blade made as it opened.

As tempting as it was to attack him then by kicking out

at him, I knew it would end in defeat. If he cried out while his companions were still nearby, they would simply rush the van before I could even cut myself free. I had to bide my time, let them get out of hearing range, and then take out this one and get to them before they could harm Amy or Ramón.

The man let out a low whistle. "Damn, you are one sweet piece."

He reached out and ripped my top off. It was just a white, sleeveless cotton T-shirt; it tore away easily as I struggled. The movements masked the effort I made to free my wrists of their bonds. Next, he tried to rip my bra in two, but the thick stitching of the middle part of the front stymied his efforts. He finally just broke the thin straps and pulled on it, until the hooks at the back gave way. He then tossed the new rag aside and gazed down at my breasts.

I asked him a question. "Do you like what you're looking at?"

"Hell yes!"

"That's good, because they're the last things you're ever going to see."

I thrust the knife under his chin and shoved it upward until the point of the blade pierced the flesh beneath his chin. As he opened his mouth to scream, I could see the long thin blade poking out of his ruptured tongue. It continued into the roof of his mouth.

He grabbed at me blindly. I had his head tilted back and his eyes were closed tight in reaction to the agony of the blade. I then twisted the knife hard, and a choked cry issued from him. It sounded more like a wheeze than a scream. Afterward, I withdrew the knife and shifted it around to cut the plastic restraints that bound my ankles. I nearly dropped it twice because my hands were slick from my attacker's blood.

It took me only a second to realize that by the time I restrained my attacker it would be too late for Amy and Ramón.

Meanwhile, the man had fallen out of the van and was crawling around in the dirt without purpose. I briefly wondered if the blade had somehow damaged his vision. In any event, he was no longer a threat.

I shuffled out of the van and searched the cab. On the passenger seat, I spied the shotgun. It was a 10 gauge with double triggers, lying beside it was the satchel full of money.

I grabbed the shotgun off the seat and used an end of it to blow the horn three times, praying that the unexpected sound would halt the planned violence taking shape out in the darkness. I scrambled beneath the van, as the sound of tentative footfalls reached my ears.

"Mike?" A voice whispered. "Mike, why did you blow the horn?"

Mike must be the name of my would-be rapist. He was wriggling near the van like a wounded worm, as a soft moan dripped from his shredded mouth.

A shape emerged from the deeper shadows, then three more. I was so happy to see that Amy and Ramón were unharmed that I nearly cried out in joy.

The first shadow grew closer. It was Derek. He had his gun out and was jerking his head this way and that when he suddenly stopped and cried out.

"Mike! Shit man, what happened?"

As he walked closer, I took aim with the shotgun and pulled hard on the right trigger. The shot caught Derek in the chest and knocked him off his feet. The recoil nearly dislocated my shoulder, caused my ears to ring, and sent my already aching head to throbbing.

As I moved out from beneath the van, Ramón headbutted Toby and sent the little man sprawling on his ass. I passed Ramón the knife as I walked over and shoved the barrel of the shotgun against Toby's stomach.

I said, "Move and you're dead." At least I think I did, with the ringing in my ears, the only word I was able to make out was "dead."

After cutting himself and Amy free, Ramón checked on Derek. He then looked over at me and shook his head. Afterward, he searched Toby for weapons and came up with my .38 and his Desert Eagle. He then took off his shirt and handed it to me. He was already a mass of bruises from the kicks he received.

"Not that I mind the view…" he said.

I snatched the shirt and wriggled into it; with all the chaos and adrenaline, I had forgotten I was topless.

Amy ran over and hugged me. "Are you all right, Aunt Blue?"

"I'm fine, baby, what about you?"

She nodded her head and pointed down at Toby. "He wouldn't let the other man hurt me."

"That's true," Ramón said. "He had just shoved the other man away from her when you blew the horn."

"Where the hell are we?" I asked Toby.

"Just south of Lubbock, off of route 87," he said.

A moan came from behind us; it was Mike. I told Toby to get to his feet and to load Mike into the back of the van. He did as I said, then Ramón secured both men with plastic restraints discovered in the glove box.

After that, I found a cell phone in a cup holder.

"Hello?"

She sounded lost.

"It's me, Becca, but hold on, someone wants to talk to you."

I passed the phone to Amy and a few moments later,

heard her say, "Don't cry, Mama, I'm fine. Aunt Blue saved me."

When Amy passed the phone back, Becca still sounded tearful.

"Thank you, Blue. Oh God, thank you."

"You're welcome, but I didn't do it alone; I had help from a mysterious stranger." I said, and sent Ramón a wink with my one good eye.

Then, the police came on the line, and I explained what had happened and told them our approximate location. They said they would send a cruiser and an ambulance to find us.

Ramón opened the satchel and looked inside.

"I don't suppose you would let me slip away with this, huh Chica?"

I smiled. "Chico, you do whatever you want."

He closed the bag up and sat it on the floor.

"Hey, Blue?"

"Yes?"

"You are one tough mama, you know that?"

I hugged Amy tighter and kissed the top of her head. "I do what I have to do."

"We all do, Chica, we all do," Ramón said, and then he leaned back against the seat and went to sleep.

PART FOUR

WHAT GOES UP?

CHAPTER 13

I was wearing a red dress and looking quite hot, if I do say so myself.

It was the kind of dress my mama would call haughty-naughty and my daddy would have never let me leave the house in.

The dress made me feel like a tart and the high heels were killing my feet, but if I wanted to blend in with my surroundings, I couldn't wear my usual jeans and boots.

I was at the premiere for an art exhibit in the richest part of Fort Worth. I was playing bodyguard to a real estate investor named Ernesto Roberts. Ernesto had recently had a dispute with a land developer named Chaney who turned out to be mob connected. Chaney was not happy how things had turned out.

Words were exchanged, threats made, and three days ago, Ernesto's car had been destroyed by a homemade bomb that detonated when Ernesto started his car remotely. Had Ernesto started the car while inside it, he would have been killed instantly.

Ernesto went to the police, and they told him that

there was nothing they could do. There was no way to prove that the car had been bombed by Chaney. They also pointed out that had Chaney been the one who wanted him dead, then maybe he should count himself lucky that Chaney had failed. The thinking being that the failed attempt would make Chaney less likely to go after him a second time, now that the cops were looking at him.

Ernesto doubted that scenario, because the land deal that he had bested Chaney on was worth over three million. The destruction of an eighty-thousand-dollar car hardly seemed to even things out.

Even though Chaney vehemently denied having anything to do with trying to kill him, Ernesto expected trouble. That's why I was by his side.

Ernesto Roberts was wearing a two-thousand-dollar tux. He was fifty-four, divorced, with hair dyed dark and a face taut from strategic nips and tucks. I was twenty-eight and wearing a sexy dress and heels while walking at his side. We looked like nearly every other couple in the place, older man, younger woman.

While playing bodyguard was not my favorite work, I did take it on occasionally if the money was right. The money was very right this time, and as the evening wore on and nothing happened, I began to think of it as easy money.

I should have known better.

When the trouble came, it had nothing to do with Ernesto. It came in the form of three armed and masked men dressed in black. The first one to enter fired a shot into the ceiling, while shouting, "Get down on the floor, now!"

When no one moved, he shot the event's lone security guard in the chest.

A second later, everyone was on the floor, and a great many of them were whimpering.

The shooter's black T-shirt had a white number 1 on the front, while the other men wore the numbers 2 and 3 on theirs.

The shooter's companions carried two duffel bags each, a red one and a blue one. As thug number 2 went right and number 3 left, we were instructed to throw our wallets and jewelry in the blue duffel and our phones in the red duffel.

I was down on the floor when thug number 2 approached Ernesto and me.

As I said, my dress was haughty-naughty, and my girls were practically spilling out of it as I lay on the floor. Even as he gathered the belongings of the people near us, I could see the bandit's eyes leering at my breasts. Meanwhile, my eyes were coveting the gun on his hip. Even from the small amount of it that I could see protruding from its holster, I could tell that it was a semi-automatic Glock possibly a model 19.

When it was our turn to hand over our belongings, I tossed my phone in the red bag and sat up on my knees. The movement not only made my breasts jiggle, but now my face was also level with the thief's crotch. As he gazed at me with a look of longing in his eyes, I reached into my purse as if to retrieve my wallet. Instead, I took out my .38 and shot him in the right leg.

The wounded man fell beside me. I used him as a shield as I yanked the gun from his holster and fired at the man who had shot the security guard. My second shot just missed hitting him in the head and he backed out into the hall.

As I ducked behind the man I had shot in the leg, I felt him tremble, even as a cry escaped him.

He had been hit by friendly fire, as the third man closed in steadily. I stuck my gun under the wounded man's chin and backed up toward the rear hallway, where the rest of the guests were already fleeing in panic.

The third man seemed to have no regard for his partner, as he kept firing in our direction. My human shield was struck at least three times, and as his knees began to buckle, I struggled to hold him in front of me.

It was a losing battle. The man outweighed me by eighty pounds, and I was still holding a gun in each hand. I let go of the man, fired off a shot, and dived behind a statue. When I peeked out to see where my assailant was, I saw him running away with the two blue bags in his hand while the red bags with the phones were sitting abandoned on the floor.

Next, I heard the ping of the elevator, but when I reached the hallway, the elevator car was already at the basement level, where the cars were parked.

I rushed back inside and stared down at the dying bandit. He was lying in a spreading puddle of blood. I reached down and pulled the hood off his head, and he gasped in pain. He was white and average-looking, but his teeth were yellow.

"Who are your partners? Where can I find them?"

"The bastard who shot me; his name is Joe Cordell."

I saw movement from the right. It was Ernesto. He was creeping toward me with a fascinated, but frightened look on his face. Behind him, men and women peeked in from the hallway, and outside, came the sound of sirens.

"And what about the other man, the one who shot the guard?"

"He... he goes by the name Jones, and you can find them at—"

The man went rigid as pain shot throughout his

midsection. I counted four separate holes in his shirt and a large tear on his left side, where an exiting bullet caused most of his blood loss. As the light faded in his eyes, he got out his final words.

"The money is hidden... in car... near... the... brakes."

And then, he died.

CHAPTER 14

THE COPS ARRESTED TWO MEN WHO WERE LEAVING THE building via the garage's exit ramp. Neither man was carrying a weapon or wearing a shirt with a number on it. One of them turned out to be Joe Cordell, who the dead crook had named as an accomplice.

Deke Thomas, a Texas Ranger and family friend, arrived on the scene and laid one of his massive hands on my shoulder.

"Hey, Blue, how you doing, girl?"

"I'm good, Deke, but the guard that got shot, how is he?"

"He's hanging in there; the paramedic says he thinks he'll make it."

He then gave me a good look and stared down his nose at me. "That's some dress, Blue."

"I was just trying to blend in while I was playing bodyguard."

"Bodyguard?"

I explained to Deke why I was there and how the

robbery went down. When I was done, he told me something that shocked me.

"Missing?" I said in surprise. "How could the bags be missing?"

"Not the bags, we found two blue duffel bags down in the garage. What we can't locate is the wallets and jewelry that was in them."

It was then that I remembered the dying man's last words.

"The one that I shot in the leg, he said that the money was hidden in a car, near the brakes."

"Yeah, that feller you were guarding, Ernesto Roberts, he said the same thing. We found nothing inside the car, but the vehicle they were using to get away is headed to the police lab. If the goods are stowed away in that car somewhere, they'll find it. We're also searching every inch of that parking garage."

Ernesto was driven home by an officer while I went to the station to make out a statement. By the time I got home, I was so drained that I took a quick shower and went right to bed.

∼

WHEN I AWOKE THE NEXT MORNING, I GOT DRESSED AND met my boyfriend Gary for breakfast at a local bistro. It was Saturday, and the weather was beautiful, so we sat outside and ate.

Although Gary was twelve years older than I was, we still meshed well and were seeing more of each other. Besides being a lawyer, Gary was also a pilot. Last month he had flown us out to the ranch he owned with his brother and sister. I got along well with the family and his ranch was beautiful. It was just the kind of spread I hoped to own someday. The one point of contention between us was my work.

"So, once again you were shot at. There's got to be a safer way to make a living, Blue, no?"

"The last time I was shot at it had nothing to do with my work as a bounty hunter and neither did this robbery. I can take care of myself, Gary, believe me."

The last time I'd been fired at, I was attempting to get my best friend Becca's young daughter back from a gang of bank robbers that had taken her as a hostage. With the help of a man named Ramón, we not only got little Amy back, but also captured the bank robbers.

Gary reached across the table and took my hand. "I know you can take care of yourself, but I still worry."

I smiled. "It's nice to know you care so much."

My phone rang; it was Deke.

"We still haven't found the loot and the lab boys stripped that car down to its frame. We've also gone over the parking garage three times and come up empty."

"That's weird, Deke. Where could they have hidden it?"

"We're still questioning them, but they're both playing dumb, which they're not. They came back positive as having gunshot residue on them; they claimed it was because they went target shooting yesterday. Get this, they weren't lying, the guys at the gun club confirmed that they were there yesterday afternoon."

"They thought of everything, but if they hid that money then you'll find it eventually."

"We're beginning to think that there was a fourth man, one that got away."

"I never saw a fourth man, but it makes sense that they might have a driver."

"One of the robbers, the one that died, he has a

younger brother with a record. We've brought him in for questioning and his apartment is being searched right now."

"Where does he say he was last night?"

"At home, with his girlfriend. She confirms it, but then, she's his girlfriend and six months pregnant. I'd think she'd say anything to keep him out of prison."

"What do you think, does he look good for it?"

"He looks like a scared kid to me. He's only twenty, got out of jail a year ago and has been working a straight job ever since. He's an elevator repairman, same job his brother had before he started doing robberies."

"Elevator repairman to armed robber, that's some career change."

"Chalk it up to drugs. The kid says his brother got hooked on meth and screwed up so much at work that they fired him. After that, he turned to crime to support his habit."

"That's messed up, Deke, but let me know if you learn anything from the brother."

"I will, and oh yeah, there's a five-thousand-dollar reward being offered now. It seems one of the pieces of jewelry, a necklace, was worth big money. If we don't locate it all soon, these fellers are gonna walk out of here with smiles on their faces."

I hung up with Deke and finished having breakfast with Gary. When we were done eating, we were going to the mall. My old laptop had died, and I was thinking about switching to a tablet. I'm not much of a shopper, but I love gadgets.

As he paid the check, Gary told me that he had to stop in at his office. He had left some papers behind that he needed to work on over the weekend. As we stood in the lobby of his office building, waiting to ride up, I had an epiphany. I suddenly realized where the robbers had stashed the loot.

∾

DEKE, ALONG WITH TWO POLICE DEPARTMENT TECH GUYS, met us at the scene of the crime.

It was the first time that Deke and Gary had met, and Deke grilled Gary as if he were my father. After my daddy went missing years ago, Deke looked out for me, my mama, and my sister as if we were his own flesh and blood.

For his part, Gary took the interrogation well and apparently passed muster, because Deke gave him a friendly slap on the back when they finished talking.

Yellow tape still stretched across the ballroom's doorway, warning all not to enter. We had no intention of entering, what we wanted was in the hallway, or so I hoped.

Deke pointed to the bank of elevators and told the lab boys to have at it.

In less than five minutes, they had found not only the jewels and wallets, but also the two numbered T-shirts and the guns. The items had been hidden in a false control panel box on the roof of the car. All of it was on top of one of the elevator cars.

Deke turned and smiled at me. "Your daddy would have been impressed, Blue, I know I am."

"Thanks, but it only made sense once you told me about the dead man's former profession. An elevator repairman would think of an elevator as an elevator car, and I remembered reading somewhere that they had brakes. So, it was worth a look."

"The kid is off the hook as an accomplice and you're five grand richer."

I smiled as I reached over and took Gary's hand. "Now we can go shopping."

When we left, we took the stairs.

PART FIVE

NORMAL LIFE

CHAPTER 15

I was seated across from Ron Tenney, owner of the AAAAAAAAA Bail Bonds Company.

Ron was in his fifties, had a full head of white hair, and a ready smile. The smile was quite a contrast to most people in this business. Dealing with criminals tended to make you sour on humanity and a frown often came easier than a grin.

Yet, Ron seemed to always be in a good mood. I suspected it was because of his wife, but having never met the woman, it was only a guess.

The AAAAAAAAA Bail Bonds Company, or Ten A, as most people called it, was in a storefront on Lancaster Avenue in Fort Worth. The building was old when Ron was born, and the office was crowded with filing cabinets and desks.

Ron handed me a flyer. "That's Joe Harmody, a bank robber; he's worth four grand if you catch him."

The man in the photo was handsome and muscular. If I hadn't known he was a bank robber, I might have guessed he was an underwear model..

"Any known associates?"

"He's a mystery, but a buddy at the county jail told me that a woman stopped in to see Harmody once. My buddy said that he's sure she was one of the waitresses at Bongo Bongo."

Bongo Bongo was a restaurant that served burgers, burgers brought to you by women in skimpy shorts and tops.

"Do you have a description of her?"

"Blonde, large breasts, and leggy, but the name on the visitors' log was Deanna Andrews."

I sat and stared at Harmody's photo. Four thousand was good money, but bank robbers tended to be violent when confronted.

Ron arched an eyebrow. "So, Blue baby, do you want it?"

I nodded. "I'll give it a week. If Harmody doesn't make contact with this Deanna Andrews by then I'll assume he's left her behind."

"Sounds like a good plan. Now, what's this I hear about you dating a defense lawyer?"

"His name is Gary Dent."

"Dent? As in *Goldman, Harper, Rogers & Dent*?"

"That's him."

"I met him once; he seemed like an okay guy."

"He is."

"Well good, but I hope it's not serious?"

"Why do you say that?"

"If you married a guy with his bucks you might quit, and you're my best bounty hunter."

I shook my head. "Oh, we're a long way from marriage."

"Not if Dent is as clever as they say he is. A smart man would scoop you up quick."

I stood and waved Harmody's picture.

"Thanks for the compliment, but right now this is the only man I'm interested in being handcuffed to."

Ron laughed. "Good hunting, Blue. And hey, be careful."

∼

Forty minutes later, I parked my pickup truck in a back corner of Bongo Bongo's parking lot. The restaurant was in a shopping center and shared the lot with a supermarket, a sporting goods store, and an electronics repair shop.

I had binoculars hanging around my neck. Whenever someone that could be Harmody walked toward the bar, I checked them out.

I had been there for two hours when my phone rang. It was Ernesto Roberts; he was the man I'd been paid to guard a week earlier.

"Mr. Roberts, how can I help you?"

"Blue? Blue there's a man here trying to get into my house. I called the police, but they haven't gotten here yet."

I started my engine as I answered him. "Is your door locked?"

"Yes, but he's kicking at it. I think he'll soon kick it open."

I was only a few minutes from Ernesto's house. I floored it as I got on the highway.

"What's the man look like?" I asked.

"He's Hispanic and very muscular. Oh God, I can see a gap in the door now."

"Stop looking at the door and run. Go out a window if you have to but get away from him and get to a neighbor's house."

"But my nearest neighbor is a half mile away."

I could hear a banging noise in the background that was accompanied by the sound of wood splintering.

"Run!" I shouted into the phone, even as I neared the exit on the highway.

When I arrived at Ernesto's, the front door was wide open. As I walked inside with my gun drawn, I heard the screaming. When I got to the rear of the house, I could see Ernesto running away from a man. The back of his large property was fenced in. Once Ernesto reached the fence, he fell against it and cowered.

I ran outside and headed straight for them. I didn't need to be stealthy; Ernesto's blubbering and begging covered the sounds of my approach.

However, Ernesto spotted me first, and the look of relief on his face made his pursuer aware that they were no longer alone. The man turned and raised his gun at me, but an instant later, he dropped his weapon to his side and smiled, as I did the same.

"Hey, Chica, what are you doing here?"

"I was going to ask you the same thing, Ramón."

"Hold on a second," Ramón said, then, he turned and knocked Ernesto senseless with one punch. Afterward, he threw him over his left shoulder and started walking back toward the house.

"Follow me, Blue, you and I have some catching up to do, eh?"

I shook my head, let out a sigh, and followed Ramón into the house.

~

When we went back inside, Ramón laid Ernesto on the sofa, then walked over to the door. Ramón closed it as best as he was able, considering that the wooden frame was splintered. When he was done, he turned and grinned at me.

"It's good to see you, but we don't have much time. There's a man coming here to kill our friend on the couch there."

"He thought you were here to kill him."

Ramón looked offended. "I'm not a killer. I find people, same as you. I was asked to find this man and—"

A motorcycle sped into the driveway. When its engine died, in the background, very faintly, I could hear an approaching siren.

Movement caught my eye and I saw Ernesto sit up on the sofa with a dazed look on his face.

The man outside got off the bike. He was dressed in black leather and wore a mirrored helmet. He took a gun out from behind his back and ran toward the door.

Ramón stood to the left of the entrance, and I took the right side. The man hit the door hard, expecting it to be locked.

When the door flew open without any resistance, he tumbled into the foyer, lost his footing, and slid across the hard wood flooring in the living room. He didn't come to rest until he was five feet from the sofa, where Ernesto, now fully awake, let out a shriek of fright.

Ramón got to the intruder first and wrest the gun from his hand, a second later, and I yanked the helmet from his head to reveal a young face with a mop of blond hair.

Ramón stared down at the man and pointed his gun at his face.

"Don't move, Chico, don't even blink."

The once faint sirens now came screaming into the circular driveway, and within seconds, the sound of the police car's doors opening reached us.

I pointed at Ramón while talking to Ernesto. "This man is your friend." I then pointed at the man on the floor. "That man is not your friend, understand?"

Ernesto nodded his head wildly. "Yes, yes, thank you, Blue, thank you for saving me."

Ramón placed a heavy boot on the back of the motorcyclist's neck and stuck the guns in his belt as I placed my gun behind my back. We had just enough time to put our hands in the air before two cops entered with their weapons drawn and ready.

CHAPTER 16

It took over five hours and eight different cops to straighten things out, but when the dust settled, Ramón and I were free, and the motorcyclist was in custody. It turned out that he was hired by the fiancé of Ernesto's niece.

The fiancé learned that Ernesto had named his niece in his will and that Ernesto had also been in a land dispute with a reputed mobster.

His plan was to kill Ernesto and frame the mobster. When the wedding took place next month, he'd be sitting pretty. However, Chaney, the mobster, learned of the hit and hired Ramón to babysit Ernesto until he could have the hit cancelled.

Needless to say, the wedding was called off.

∼

Ramón and I were sitting in Bongo Bongo. We were both eating one of their famed Bongo burgers. The interior of the place was brightly lit and there were TVs everywhere with sporting events playing on them.

And while the shorts and tops of the waitresses were revealing, they weren't as skimpy as I'd imagined they would be.

Ramón watched as a particularly well-endowed waitress walked by, then he smiled at me.

"I'm surprised you picked this place to grab a bite, but I have no complaints."

"I'm working. There's a bail skip who might show here. I figured why not kill two birds with one stone."

"How is my little Amy?"

"She's good; Becca says she still talks about you."

"Tell Amy I said hi when you see her."

"Actually, Becca's been bugging me to bring you to dinner one night; she and her husband Richie want to thank you personally for saving Amy."

Ramón blanched.

"What?" I asked.

"I'm not used to normal people wanting to spend time with me, that's all."

"What do you mean normal? You're not normal?"

"Both my parents died when I was still a boy and after that I was a gangbanger. I broke free from that life and have been on my own ever since."

"Don't you have any other family?"

"Yeah, I have some blood relatives, but we never talk."

"What about friends?"

He shook his head. "I consider myself your friend," I said.

"Thank you, Chica, Blue; that means a lot to me."

"So, when can I tell Becca to expect you?"

"Never. Whenever I get around normal people it makes me nervous. I can't imagine working nine to five and then coming home to the same woman night after night, and the kids, all that responsibility, it isn't natural."

"I think you're an adrenaline junkie, but I warn you, I promised Becca that I'd bring you by someday, and I never break a promise."

He grinned. "This one might be your first."

"So how long have you worked for Chaney?"

"I don't. I'm freelance. If you want somebody found; I'll find them. The bodyguard bit today was a one-time thing. So, who's this guy you're looking for?"

I told Ramón about Joe Harmody and his connection to Bongo Bongo.

"Four grand? That's good money, but if he's smart, he won't come back here."

"Yeah, I know, but I—"

"Gotta check it out," Ramón finished.

I laughed. "That's right."

"You got a picture of this guy?"

I passed him a copy of the flyer with Harmody's photo on it and he studied it.

"Bank robbers are short term thinkers, every one of them. There was a guy in California years ago who robbed banks for twenty years and got away with over three million. When they finally caught him, he had less than a thousand dollars to his name."

Our waitress came by and asked if we needed anything else. She had big blonde hair, obvious fake boobs and long, shapely legs. I told her that we were good and asked for the bill. Before she left the table, she sent Ramón a bright and lingering smile.

"It looks like our waitress likes you."

"All women find me irresistible; in fact, it's probably taking all of your self-control not to reach across the table and fondle me."

"The thought has crossed my mind, but I'm seeing someone."

"That guy Gary you told me about?"

"Yes."

"Good for him. Now tell me, which of these girls is Harmody's?"

The waitress walked back toward us with our bill in her hand and her eyes on Ramón.

"Here she comes now," I said.

~

At closing time, Ramón left the restaurant with our waitress, otherwise known as Deanna Andrews. He was going to try to get her to open up about Harmody. I appreciated the assistance but doubted that his only motive was to help me; after all, Deanna Andrews was a good-looking woman. I don't mind saying that I envied her. Ramón was a good-looking man.

I followed them to her apartment and searched the street for any sign of Harmody. There was none. It was quiet, after two a.m., and the street was deserted.

A light came on in a third-floor apartment and a second later, went off. I thought it odd, but harmless, that is, until I saw the two struggling figures bang against the window.

I jumped from my truck and raced up the stairs to the third floor. Just as I rounded the corner, a shot rang out, followed by a man yelling, "No!"

I tried the door and found that it was unlocked. As I eased it open, Ramón called my name.

"Blue?"

"It's me."

I found the light switch.

Joe Harmody was on his knees in the middle of the living room and crying in grief. Lying on the floor beside him was Deanna Andrews. There was a gunshot wound that entered just beneath her right eye. There was no need to try for a pulse, the brains and blood splattered about the room told me she was dead.

"What happened?"

Ramón looked a bit shaken, but his voice was strong and unwavering.

"When we entered, I hit the lights and she shut them off and kissed me. I heard a sound behind me and found Harmody coming at me. He had a gun in one hand and a blackjack in the other. I threw his partner, Deanna, at him, and reached for my gun. As I was taking it out, she grabbed my wrist and we struggled for a second before I could throw her off me. As I pushed her away, Harmody fired a shot at me and hit her instead. When he realized what he'd done, he dropped the gun and rushed over to her."

A tentative knock came at the door. I opened it to find an elderly woman wearing a pink robe. In the hallway behind her were other people in their sleepwear.

"I heard a shot. Is Deanna all right?"

I sighed. "No ma'am, please call the police."

The old woman began to cry.

"I already called."

～

ALTHOUGH RAMÓN MIGHT BE IRRESISTIBLE, DEANNA Andrews took him home that night because he was roughly Harmody's height and size. They had planned to lure someone to her apartment and murder them.

Afterward, they would place the corpse in Harmody's

car and set the vehicle ablaze. It was to be an attempt to fake Harmody's death, and to then start a new life together.

Instead, Deanna was dead and Harmody was going to spend the rest of his life behind bars.

∼

Ramón insisted on bringing wine because, as he put it, "That's what real people do, right?"

When Becca answered the door with Richie, Amy pushed her way out between them and jumped up into Ramón's arms.

"Ramón, I missed you," Amy said, then she gave him a big smooch on the lips.

Ramón smiled at me. "Maybe normal life isn't so bad after all."

Then, we entered the house and had dinner with our friends.

PART SIX

THE MONSTER IN THE WOODS

CHAPTER 17

I was in East Texas, deep inside the Piney Woods.

The Piney Woods are fifty thousand square miles of forest that stretch across parts of four states. I was there looking for a bail skip named Tanner Harlow. Harlow was a doctor, forty-nine, long divorced and, judging by his picture, would appear to look younger than his age.

Dr. Harlow had embezzled over two million dollars from the medical facility he was employed at. He did so after learning that they planned to sever ties with him. That same night, he was arrested for driving while intoxicated.

He managed to bail himself out on the drunk driving charge just in time to be arrested for the embezzlement. Two days later, he skipped on an eighty-thousand-dollar bond and left Fort Worth.

After asking around, I discovered that Harlow was an avid hiker and often spent time in the Piney Woods while on vacation.

Seven hours of driving got me to the woods. After talking to dozens of people, I came across a man who knew Harlow slightly. He told me that he had spotted the doctor earlier that day, hiking along a trail that led into Louisiana.

That made sense: Harlow was from Louisiana and still had family there.

I contacted the local cops and let them know who I was and who I was after. I soon met with a Forest Ranger named Doug Selby. Selby greeted me with a smile and a tip of his cap, before asking me to hop into his yellow Jeep.

Selby was about my age and wore a wedding band. He had a full head of reddish-blonde hair that seemed to go in all directions at once.

After we chatted up some people at a campsite, we learned that a man fitting Dr. Harlow's description had been seen hiking along a trail less than a mile from where we were.

Selby and I hopped back into the Jeep and drove parallel to the trail for about five miles. Afterward, we parked the Jeep amid a copse of trees. After I put my backpack on, we then walked northwest along the trail and hoped to run right into Harlow.

As we tramped along, Selby and I talked quietly.

"Is this guy supposed to be dangerous?" he asked.

"No, he's a doctor, an obstetrician, but then, you never can tell."

"I hear you, so how long have you been a bail enforcer?"

I opened my mouth to answer him when Tanner Harlow came walking out from behind a bush while zipping up his fly. I grabbed the cuffs off my belt and walked over to him.

"Dr. Tanner Harlow, you are under arrest for the crime of—"

And that's when he turned and ran back into the

woods.

Selby and I shared a look of frustration, then we went after him. Harlow was in good shape, but he was still twenty years older than either me or Selby. We ran him down within minutes and I cuffed his hands behind his back.

Thank God Selby was along. Harlow's attempt at escape had taken us deep into the woods on a meandering route. I could only guess where we'd left the Jeep. Without hesitation, Selby pointed north and began guiding us back to the trail.

While walking back, we heard a noise that sounded like someone digging. Selby motioned for me to stay put with Harlow, before he moved quietly toward the sound to take a look. A few seconds later, I heard him shouting.

"You! Drop that shovel and put your hands in the air. Now!"

The next thing I knew, several shots were fired from two different guns.

With my weapon in my hand, I ran toward the sound of the shots while dragging Harlow along by the belt. He tripped and fell on his face just as I spotted a strange man reloading his weapon.

The guy was six feet tall, with a thirty-something face and prematurely white hair. He stood over Selby, who was wounded and writhing in pain on the ground.

Twenty feet to the Selby's left was the body of a naked girl, lying in the dirt. One look at her lineless, bloodless face and I knew two things. One: she was dead. And two: she had never made it beyond fourteen years of age.

I told the man to drop his weapon just as he finished reloading. He raised his gun and I shot at him three times, but missed, due to the distance. The man turned and ran into the trees.

I rushed over to Selby and saw that he had been struck once in the abdomen, but that there was no exit wound. As Selby gritted his teeth against the pain, I grabbed the radio from his belt and reached the dispatcher at his headquarters.

It was only then that I realized I had little idea how to tell them where to find us. I'm no city slicker, but the Piney Woods were unfamiliar to me. That fact was the main reason Selby was along in the first place.

He must have realized this too, because he motioned for me to place the radio near his mouth so that he could talk.

It took over a minute, but between moans and gasps of pain, Selby let his fellow Rangers know where we were, and that his attacker was extremely dangerous.

Harlow!

I had forgotten all about him. I turned my head and found that he was still lying where he fell, eyes wide and staring at the dead girl with a look of horror on his face.

I rushed over to him, helped him to stand, and took off the handcuffs.

"Ranger Selby's been shot, help him."

"What?"

"You're a doctor, help him."

"I don't do gunshots; I deliver babies."

I shoved him toward Selby. "Help him!"

A scream.

It was followed by two shots, then silence.

I picked Selby's gun up from the ground before taking my backpack off and tossing it to Harlow.

"I know it's not much, but there's a first-aid kit and bottled water in there. You do what you can to help him. When the other Rangers arrive, tell them that there may be more casualties west of here."

I was thirty feet away when Harlow called to me.

"Where are you going?"

"I'm going after the killer."

I headed toward the place where the screams came from while praying that Dr. Harlow would help Selby and not run away again.

The woods were thick with fallen branches, and I soon gave up any attempt at stealth. Every step cracked and crunched fallen twigs and leaves, and so I relied on my eyes to keep me safe.

If anything moved, I would be ready to kill it.

I found the source of the scream lying at the side of a trail with a gaping wound in the back of her head, beside her lay an older man with features much like her own. He had probably been her father. He'd been shot in the heart and must have died instantly.

As I moved past them, I noticed blood on the man's right fingertips, a closer look revealed what looked like flesh.

Good!

He had marked the son of a bitch even as he died. When I caught the monster, he wouldn't be able to deny the DNA evidence under the nails of his victim.

From my right and below, I heard someone traipsing through the woods, and I headed that way.

A few minutes later, I came upon a dirt road that was nearly hidden by foliage, then I heard an engine start a hundred yards to my left.

I cursed. Of course, he had a car nearby. He couldn't very well have walked the dead girl in here on foot.

A moment later, I saw the car. It was a black BMW, and it was picking up speed. I ran into the road and fired a shot into the air, before sighting in on the windshield.

The killer ducked down just as he floored the car. I

leapt aside and waited. When he was even with me, I fired my gun's two remaining shots at the right front tire and watched as the car swerved toward the trees.

He hit a stand of saplings with a resounding *CLUNK!* that caused steam to rise from under the hood, but a moment later, he was out of the car and sprinting away.

He was fast, faster than me by far. As we reached a treeless field of weeds, he was nearly a city block ahead of me.

My gun was empty, but I still had Ranger Selby's *Colt Python*. I checked the cylinder, three bullets left.

I fell to one knee, arms extended, and sighted down the six-inch barrel.

My first shot missed, but the sound of it halted him and he stared back at me.

Big mistake.

I fired a second shot and watched him jerk his head back with a start. Then, he reached up to the right side of his head. Even from where I was, I could see the blood on his fingers.

He shouted a string of obscenities and began firing at me in a frenzy.

I hit the ground hard and, and as cliché as it sounds, I heard the bullets whiz above my head.

Click! Click! Click!

He was empty. I raised my head. We locked eyes for a moment before he dropped the now useless gun and ran away.

I followed, with one bullet and one thought, to stop this walking nightmare before he hurt anyone else.

The field ended at a small stream. As I reached it, I saw him on the opposite bank. I splashed my way across while keeping him in sight. When I was halfway to the other side my foot landed on something slimy and I went down on one knee. I felt an immediate jolt of pain as my right knee landed on a jagged rock and cut through my jeans. When I reached the shore, I was wet up to my waist and had a scraped, bloody knee, but the pain was fading, and I was still able to run.

I looked around for my prey. Just when I thought I had lost him, I spotted a shock of white hair running away to my right. His hair was so white that it was brilliant and seemed to sparkle whenever the sun hit it.

I then followed him as best as I could. It was a losing proposition though, as he was just faster than I was, and soon I lost sight of him amidst the thickening trees.

I slowed, listening for footfalls, for movement, for anything.

When the silence broke, it was so loud and so close that I nearly leapt out of my skin.

"What the hell are you doin' there, son?"

The question came from an old man sitting up in a tree, in a deer blind. He was looking down at a tree ten feet in front of me. My white-haired quarry stepped out of his hiding place and threw something up at the old man.

I saw a glint of metal, a flash of blood, and then the old man tumbled twenty feet to the ground with a knife in his throat.

I fired my last remaining shot at White Hair as he reached down to pull the rifle off the dying old man.

White hair screamed in pain and left the rifle. I watched as he hobbled off into the woods and knew he'd been wounded. I ran to the old hunter to see if I could help, but he had already died from either the fall or the knife in his throat.

Four dead bodies and a seriously wounded Ranger in less than an hour, White Hair needed to be stopped, and he needed to be stopped now.

I relieved the dead hunter of his rifle and was happy to see that it had a scope. It was a Weatherby with a twenty-eight-inch barrel. My daddy had one just like it when I was growing up. I'd shot it enough to know how to use it.

I followed White Hair and was pleased to see an intermittent blood trail amongst the grass. Within a minute, I was in sight of him as we came upon a hill that sloped downward. The hill ended at what sounded like a road, as the sound of tires on pavement came and went sporadically.

My last bullet had slowed White Hair down, and as he reached the rim of the slope, I was less than a hundred feet behind him.

He went down the tall hill in an uncontrollable slide and hit bottom hard before tumbling out into the road. A green Mercedes braked with a long squeal and just avoided running him over. When it finally stopped, he was lying halfway beneath it.

The driver of the car, a well-dressed, middle-aged woman with short red hair, exited the car. As I cried out to warn her, White Hair leapt up and punched her in the face.

The woman fell to the ground, unconscious, and White Hair ran around to the driver's side door. He stared up at me then with a maniacal grin on his scratched and bloody face as he sent me an obscene gesture.

As he sat in the driver's seat, I dropped flat, rifle up, and sighted down at him.

Before I could take the shot, he floored the gas pedal and drove over the woman lying in the road. He deliberately aimed for her head, and he hit it.

I dropped the rifle in revulsion as I fought to not vomit at what the car had done to her.

Then, rage overcame repulsion, and I grabbed the rifle

again.

By the time I took the first shot, he was a quarter of a mile away, moving fast, and it was a downward angle.

I missed, not even close.

The second shot brought the sound of breaking glass to my ears, but the car stayed on the road and was approaching a curve.

Time was running out.

I had three cartridges left and I let all three fly.

My reward was the sight of a splattered, bloody window and the beautiful vision of the car swerving into a ditch and flipping over, end over end.

I then laid the rifle down on the grass and cried.

I was still lying there when I heard the police and ambulance arrive below, and a few moments later, a helicopter appeared overhead.

It landed in the field behind me, and a State Trooper walked toward me, walking beside him was Dr. Tanner Harlow.

"Blue Steele?" the trooper said.

I nodded.

"I'm State Trooper, Sergeant John Wincomb. Ranger Selby is on his way to the hospital. He's going to make it, thanks to Dr. Harlow here."

I looked over at Harlow. "Thank you."

Harlow shrugged. "I was a doctor before I was a thief. I would never just run away and let a man die."

Wincomb pointed at the rifle slung over my shoulder. "You got him with that?"

"Yes."

"That's some fine shooting."

"I want to go home," I said.

Wincomb nodded in understanding, and the three of us headed for the chopper.

BLUE RETURNS!

BLUE STEELE - BROKEN - BOOK 2

AFTERWORD

Thank you,

REMINGTON KANE

JOIN MY INNER CIRCLE

You'll receive FREE books, such as,

SLAY BELLS – A TANNER NOVEL – BOOK 0

TAKEN! ALPHABET SERIES – 26 ORIGINAL TAKEN! TALES

BLUE STEELE - KARMA

Also – Exclusive short stories featuring TANNER, along with other books.

TO BECOME AN INNER CIRCLE MEMBER, GO TO:

http://remingtonkane.com/mailing-list/

ALSO BY REMINGTON KANE

The TANNER Series in order

INEVITABLE I - A Tanner Novel - Book 1

KILL IN PLAIN SIGHT - A Tanner Novel - Book 2

MAKING A KILLING ON WALL STREET - A Tanner Novel - Book 3

THE FIRST ONE TO DIE LOSES - A Tanner Novel - Book 4

THE LIFE & DEATH OF CODY PARKER - A Tanner Novel - Book 5

WAR - A Tanner Novel- A Tanner Novel - Book 6

SUICIDE OR DEATH - A Tanner Novel - Book 7

TWO FOR THE KILL - A Tanner Novel - Book 8

BALLET OF DEATH - A Tanner Novel - Book 9

MORE DANGEROUS THAN MAN - A Tanner Novel - Book 10

TANNER TIMES TWO - A Tanner Novel - Book 11

OCCUPATION: DEATH - A Tanner Novel - Book 12

HELL FOR HIRE - A Tanner Novel - Book 13

A HOME TO DIE FOR - A Tanner Novel - Book 14

FIRE WITH FIRE - A Tanner Novel - Book 15

TO KILL A KILLER - A Tanner Novel - Book 16

WHITE HELL – A Tanner Novel - Book 17

MANHATTAN HIT MAN – A Tanner Novel - Book 18

ONE HUNDRED YEARS OF TANNER – A Tanner Novel -

Book 19

REVELATIONS - A Tanner Novel - Book 20

THE SPY GAME - A Tanner Novel - Book 21

A VICTIM OF CIRCUMSTANCE - A Tanner Novel - Book 22

A MAN OF RESPECT - A Tanner Novel - Book 23

THE MAN, THE MYTH - A Tanner Novel - Book 24

ALL-OUT WAR - A Tanner Novel - Book 25

THE REAL DEAL - A Tanner Novel - Book 26

WAR ZONE - A Tanner Novel - Book 27

ULTIMATE ASSASSIN - A Tanner Novel - Book 28

KNIGHT TIME - A Tanner Novel - Book 29

PROTECTOR - A Tanner Novel - Book 30

BULLETS BEFORE BREAKFAST - A Tanner Novel - Book 31

VENGEANCE - A Tanner Novel - Book 32

TARGET: TANNER - A Tanner Novel - Book 33

BLACK SHEEP - A Tanner Novel - Book 34

FLESH AND BLOOD - A Tanner Novel - Book 35

NEVER SEE IT COMING - A Tanner Novel - Book 36

MISSING - A Tanner Novel - Book 37

CONTENDER - A Tanner Novel - Book 38

TO SERVE AND PROTECT - A Tanner Novel - Book 39

STALKING HORSE - A Tanner Novel - Book 40

THE EVIL OF TWO LESSERS - A Tanner Novel - Book 41

SINS OF THE FATHER AND MOTHER - A Tanner Novel - Book 42

SOULLESS - A Tanner Novel - Book 43

LIT FUSE - A Tanner Novel - Book 44
HYENAS - A Tanner Novel - Book 45
MANHUNT - A Tanner Novel - Book 46
IN FOR THE KILL - A Tanner Novel - Book 47

The Young Guns Series in order

YOUNG GUNS
YOUNG GUNS 2 - SMOKE & MIRRORS
YOUNG GUNS 3 - BEYOND LIMITS
YOUNG GUNS 4 - RYKER'S RAIDERS
YOUNG GUNS 5 - ULTIMATE TRAINING
YOUNG GUNS 6 - CONTRACT TO KILL
YOUNG GUNS 7 - FIRST LOVE
YOUNG GUNS 8 - THE END OF THE BEGINNING

A Tanner Series in order

TANNER: YEAR ONE
TANNER: YEAR TWO
TANNER: YEAR THREE
TANNER: YEAR FOUR
TANNER: YEAR FIVE

The TAKEN! Series in order

TAKEN! - LOVE CONQUERS ALL - Book 1
TAKEN! - SECRETS & LIES - Book 2
TAKEN! - STALKER - Book 3
TAKEN! - BREAKOUT! - Book 4

TAKEN! - THE THIRTY-NINE - Book 5
TAKEN! - KIDNAPPING THE DEVIL - Book 6
TAKEN! - HIT SQUAD - Book 7
TAKEN! - MASQUERADE - Book 8
TAKEN! - SERIOUS BUSINESS - Book 9
TAKEN! - THE COUPLE THAT SLAYS TOGETHER - Book 10
TAKEN! - PUT ASUNDER - Book 11
TAKEN! - LIKE BOND, ONLY BETTER - Book 12
TAKEN! - MEDIEVAL - Book 13
TAKEN! - RISEN! - Book 14
TAKEN! - VACATION - Book 15
TAKEN! - MICHAEL - Book 16
TAKEN! - BEDEVILED - Book 17
TAKEN! - INTENTIONAL ACTS OF VIOLENCE - Book 18
TAKEN! - THE KING OF KILLERS – Book 19
TAKEN! - NO MORE MR. NICE GUY - Book 20 & the Series Finale

The MR. WHITE Series

PAST IMPERFECT - MR. WHITE - Book 1
HUNTED - MR. WHITE - Book 2

The UNLEASH Series

TERROR IN NEW YORK - Book 1
THE EXECUTIONER'S MASK - Book 2

The BLUE STEELE Series in order

BLUE STEELE - BOUNTY HUNTER- Book 1
BLUE STEELE - BROKEN- Book 2
BLUE STEELE - VENGEANCE- Book 3
BLUE STEELE - THAT WHICH DOESN'T KILL ME- Book 4
BLUE STEELE - ON THE HUNT- Book 5
BLUE STEELE - PAST SINS - Book 6
BLUE STEELE - DADDY'S GIRL - Book 7 & the Series Finale

The CALIBER DETECTIVE AGENCY Series in order

CALIBER DETECTIVE AGENCY - GENERATIONS- Book 1
CALIBER DETECTIVE AGENCY - TEMPTATION- Book 2
CALIBER DETECTIVE AGENCY - A RANSOM PAID IN BLOOD- Book 3
CALIBER DETECTIVE AGENCY - MISSING- Book 4
CALIBER DETECTIVE AGENCY - DECEPTION- Book 5
CALIBER DETECTIVE AGENCY - CRUCIBLE- Book 6
CALIBER DETECTIVE AGENCY – LEGENDARY – Book 7
CALIBER DETECTIVE AGENCY – WE ARE GATHERED HERE TODAY - Book 8
CALIBER DETECTIVE AGENCY - MEANS, MOTIVE, and OPPORTUNITY - Book 9 & the Series Finale

THE TAKEN!/TANNER Series in order

THE CONTRACT: KILL JESSICA WHITE - Taken!/Tanner - Book 1
UNFINISHED BUSINESS – Taken!/Tanner – Book 2

THE ABDUCTION OF THOMAS LAWSON - Taken!/Tanner – Book 3

PREDATOR - Taken!/Tanner - Book 4

DETECTIVE PIERCE Series in order

MONSTERS - A Detective Pierce Novel - Book 1

DEMONS - A Detective Pierce Novel - Book 2

ANGELS - A Detective Pierce Novel - Book 3

THE OCEAN BEACH ISLAND Series in order

THE MANY AND THE ONE - Book 1

SINS & SECOND CHANES - Book 2

DRY ADULTERY, WET AMBITION -Book 3

OF TONGUE AND PEN - Book 4

ALL GOOD THINGS… - Book 5

LITTLE WHITE SINS - Book 6

THE LIGHT OF DARKNESS - Book 7

STERN ISLAND - Book 8 & the Series Finale

THE REVENGE Series in order

JOHNNY REVENGE - The Revenge Series - Book 1

THE APPOINTMENT KILLER - The Revenge Series - Book 2

AN I FOR AN I - The Revenge Series - Book 3

ALSO

THE EFFECT: Reality is changing!

THE FIX-IT MAN: A Tale of True Love and Revenge

DOUBLE OR NOTHING

PARKER & KNIGHT

REDEMPTION: Someone's taken her

DESOLATION LAKE

TIME TRAVEL TALES & OTHER SHORT STORIES

BLUE STEELE – BOUNTY HUNTER
Copyright © REMINGTON KANE, 2013
YEAR ZERO PUBLISHING

This book is a work of fiction. Names, characters, places and incidents either are products of the author's imagination or are used fictitiously.

Any resemblance to actual events or locales or persons, living or dead, is entirely coincidental.

All rights reserved. Except as permitted under the U.S. Copyright Act of 1976, no part of this publication may be reproduced, distributed or transmitted in any form or by any means, or stored in a database or retrieval system, without the prior written permission of the publisher.

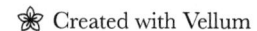

❦ Created with Vellum

Made in the USA
Columbia, SC
03 December 2022